Whispers from the East

Amie Ali

Green Garnet Books

Whispers from the East

Copyright
First published in the United States in 2015 by Green Garnet
Books.
Copyright © Amie Ali 2015
The moral right of the author has been asserted.

ISBN: 0692385142
ISBN-13: 978-0692385142

For Daddy.

"The great man is he who does not lose his child's heart." ~ Mencius

CONTENTS

Acknowledgements

Enormous thanks belong first and foremost to my esteemed mentor, BHH, who held my hand and offered kindness and constructive criticism in the writing of this manuscript.

To Paula, Lisa, Kelly, Mandy, Amanda, and Rebekah, whose lives, stories, and friendship inspire me and help maintain my threadbare sanity in everyday living.

To my parents, siblings, family, and friends— my circle of trust—I love you all.

And finally, to my husband and daughter, who have lovingly tolerated years of being dragged to obscure cities, sites, and museums. We might wander the planet together but, even if we weren't able to, you two mean the entire world to me.

Prologue

Drawing in a deep, exhausted breath, Iqra took the seat next to Ivy on the burgundy sofa. The chaise lounge of Ammi, their mother-in-law, had sat empty, waiting to be filled since she had fallen out of it six days before in the first of a series of heart attacks.

Abbu, their father-in-law, had his own ideas regarding the cause.

"She carried the stress of the entire family," he said. "Her heart just gave out."

Three weeks before she collapsed, Ivy and Ammi had spoken on the phone, and she relayed her concern about another daughter-in-law, Carolyn, committing apostasy by leaving Islam and rejoining her prior faith, Christianity.

"Nazar will have to divorce her," Ammi stated matter of factly.

"She's pregnant, Ammi," Ivy replied softly, attempting to mitigate through the gale of a hopeless situation.

"Too hard for the children. Too hard for everyone."

Ammi had declared that Carolyn and Nazar's son and the child on the way would be confused about religion. Ivy believed she was right but could see no way to resolve the situation in a compassionate and balanced way, preserving a family while still upholding their faith. Her mind wandered to the questions her lips couldn't. *A child born into Islam is instructed to hold his mother in the highest regard—above all others—without question. When one's mother is of another religion, it seems impossible that a son could do this and still uphold other binding conditions of the faith. How do you keep the status of a mother elevated when her beliefs not only contradict your own, but guide the very task of raising you? And how does a child grow up a strong Muslim with a mother who tells him to pray to Jesus, peace be upon him?*

The situation was unbearably muddled.

A Pakistani mother fears that her son might one day reach outside the cocoon of culture to pick a bride himself, foregoing her consent and disregarding age-old customs that bind a family. The horror of this prospect is compounded exponentially when the bride of his choosing is a non-Muslim *gori* from the West. This depravity, this unspeakable action by a son, had become a reality in Ammi's life. Not just with one precious boy, but two.

A Bottle of Oil

Some time ago, a poor man lived in a house beside the home of a wealthy merchant who sold oil and honey. The Merchant was an exceedingly kind neighbor, and one day sent a flask of oil over to the poor man. Delighted, the poor man placed it carefully away on a top shelf of an old curio cabinet. That evening as he was gazing at it, he said half aloud,

"I wonder how much oil there is in that bottle? There is a large quantity. If I should sell it, I could buy five sheep. Every year I should have lambs, and before long I should own a whole flock. Then I should sell some of the sheep and be rich enough to marry a wife. Perhaps we might have a son! And what a fine boy he would be! So tall, strong, and obedient! But if he should disobey me..." and he raised the staff which he held in his hand, "...I should punish him thus!" he swung the staff over his head and brought it down heavily to the ground, knocking the base of the curio. As he did so, the flask tumbled from the shelf, the oil spilled forward and ran over him from head to foot.

Chapter 1

Ammi
1947 - Lahore, Pakistan

Ammi settled in Lahore in 1947 following the
partition of India that made Pakistan a sovereign
country, and on the eve of her twenty-fourth birthday.
That year, Ammi and Abbu left India with more than
seven million other Muslims, taking part in the greatest
cross migration the world had ever witnessed. Her belly
fat with their first son, they made the arduous journey

armed with little more than a few bulky suitcases, Ammi's gold jewelry, and the hope of a better life in the religious majority. They reached the house of Abbu's brother unscathed eight days before Safwat emerged from the womb.

"You were born when many around us were dying," Ammi would whisper into baby Safwat's ear, as he wrapped his tiny fingers through the gold bangles strung up her bronzed arm.

"I had had visions of Lahore before I had ever seen it," she confessed to her infant son, in the hope that breathing the words onto her child might somehow help her finally accept they had happened. "I imagined the *adhaans* beckoning the faithful to prayers, ladies dressed modestly without the indecency of a flesh-flashing sari, and the safety and freedom to practice Islam in a properly Muslim country."

The Lahore she came to had all of this, but was also besieged with the tattered and mutilated men, women, and children who had not experienced as smooth a journey as she. Displaced refugees spilled into the city having entered it starving, their possessions stolen, no family or homes to shelter them, and the virtue of their women violently sacrificed. Wailing mothers wandered the streets begging for news of missing daughters whose husbands arrived bloody and without their wives. Riots and theft were trivial to those making the migration, one where kidnap, rape, and massacres were frequent and widespread.

Although they had made it safely themselves, there was no immunity when the bloody fingers of misfortune reached into their extended family.

"Little Safwat." She continued to stare down at him, willing the baby to make eye contact. "Your second cousin, Kyda, she was lost in all this. Only seven years old, practically a baby herself." She pinched his nose with her finger, causing him to gurgle and sneeze. He looked up with eager eyes, and she knew she had his attention.

"Your sweet cousin's train left only four short hours after your Abbu and mine departed New Delhi. We all waited at the station eager to see her step off with her parents. Eighteen hours late, it finally came, and *jaanu*, we were so excited!"

Safwat giggled, forming bubbles on his mouth. Ammi took a corner of her soft blue *dupatta* to wipe away his spittle.

"They opened the doors to the carriages, and the smell that rolled off that train, I couldn't describe it even if I were the great poet Faiz Ahmad Faiz himself."

Safwat's mouth opened wide in a yawn. She leaned her head back against the headboard, too tired from thinking of it to continue.

Only the men on the train had arrived, all of them cold, dead, and disfigured. Kyda and her mother had vanished. The body of Kyda's father, barely recognizable, had been pulled off and laid just beside the tracks in the row after row of mangled corpses ready to be identified and collected. They later learned from a solitary female survivor that at a stop in Amritsar, the train was ambushed by a faction of rebels. Women were dragged out of compartments, their children pulled from hiding places under the bunks. Nobody was spared the brutality of the ensuing massacre, save this single Muslim woman who had done the unspeakable act of tattooing the Lord Krishna on her arm and successfully passed herself off as a Hindu convert, creating a story to her would-be captors that she was forced onto the train by her family. The ingenuity of her planning in the hours leading to the partition may have temporarily spared her physical life, but as a Muslim, she was outcast and soon

9

after killed as an idolater and apostate. The dead men and lost women were honored for courage and martyrdom by their grieving families and an entire nation. Ammi knew that she and Abbu had been fortunate in their circumstances leading up to the partition, even if it was the result of a heartbreaking loss.

With the recent passing of Abbu's mother, who was also Ammi's aunt, her small New Delhi house and heavy gold jewelry were quickly sold to a newly settled Hindu merchant eager to make the purchase. The house's furnishings were a part of the sale, leaving Ammi and Abbu with little to carry and the means to purchase train tickets. It was their ability to take off quickly in the earliest, most fleeting moments before the mass exodus began that allowed them to arrive in Lahore unharmed.

Despite all the blood and turmoil raging outside their front door, settling into her brother-in-law's Lahori house was not in itself difficult.

"We will all be a family once more," Imran said, clasping hands with his younger brother. "We will never, any of us, be separated again, *inshaAllah*."

He was as eager to meet his new nephew as he would've been a son of his own, had he been blessed with one, he told them. Fatima, his wife and Ammi's sister, had given him a daughter, Iqra, two years before Ammi's arrival. The birth had been difficult, and Fatima had been told soon after that Iqra would likely be an only child. Fatima and Imran both prayed fervently for Allah to bless them with more children, but when no more came, they devoted all their love and energy to the beautiful girl they had.

Fatima had taken Ammi into her arms, and she felt the immediate, familiar comfort of her older sister's embrace. "You are here now," she said. "You will be safe, *inshaAllah*."

It had forever been the custom of the subcontinent for parents to arrange marriages among the children of their siblings. The honor and preservation of the family, its values, and customs were the driving force behind marriage, along with that family's growth and the strengthening of familial bonds. The birth of Safwat meant the same to both doting sets of parents. Iqra was assured a good husband raised in the home of her parents, and Safwat would have a respectable, righteous wife groomed as such by her mother and aunt, who would in the future be her mother-in-law. Partitioning the countries robbed many families of every material possession and dignity they had, but the

11

tradition and rites of Islamic living created the foundation that would hold firm and help cobble the loss of humanity back together.

Ammi and Abbu's marriage was the end result of this established custom, as was Fatima and Imran's. Fatima and Ammi, sisters, married their first cousins on their father's side—Abbu and Imran, who were brothers. The West generally considered this entanglement sordid, even incestuous. In the East, it had always been a delicate thread that wove together the fabric of a family, a community, a society, an entire way of life. Instrumental in a religion that did not permit any form of courtship, it left matrimonial matters in the capable and practical hands of parents.

Imran installed Abbu in a middle-management position at the packaging company he had taken over prior to the partition. It had been owned by a Sikh preparing to make the opposite migration out of Pakistan. Business was beginning to flourish, and the brothers were able to secure contracts with new vendors who had become overnight business owners in the same fashion. Pooling resources, in less than a year, they could afford to move their family together from the small house in Lahore's Johar Town to a larger home in the chic residential district of Gulberg, right in the heart of the city.

The home was a sufficient in size to comfortably house the growing family of six, a housemaid, and a guard at their small front gate. Split over three levels, it boasted an entry with a large white marble foyer and a sweeping, curved sandalwood staircase leading to the living rooms upstairs. A modernized kitchen to the right of the grand foyer was sealed off by a heavy door meant to conceal both its contents and the layered smells of grease and heady curries that would otherwise plague a Pakistani home. The kitchen possessed a brand new Wedgewood stove, imported from England, complete with a built-in single oven, broiler, griddle, four gas burners, and a warming drawer.

Its contemporary white porcelain-and-enamel façade stood in stark contrast to the traditional clay oven that lay adjacent to it. A slick, fast-talking salesman spent seven days teaching the maid how to use the modern contraption, after which it stood untouched.

At about sixty years of age, the guard standing attention at the gate was placed less for security and more as a status symbol of the family's upward movement onto the fringes of Lahore's social society.

While the old caste system of India had been deemed unislamic and purged politically from Pakistan, its undercurrents still rippled through the classes of the Punjab and carried on the framework of a long structured social hierarchy. With the surname *Miah*, Ammi, Abbu, Fatima, Imran and their children were bound securely within the upper middle class without having done anything significant outside the good fortune of being born with such a name.

On one hot afternoon, Fatima offered a plate brimming with crescent-shaped, sweet mango slices to Ammi.

"Here, have a slice."

Ammi waved her hand, gesturing the plate away and readjusted herself on the burgundy sofa. It was still wrapped in the plastic it had been delivered in two years before. Her thick black braid settled over her shoulder, stretching down to the waist of her brightly colored pink and green floral *kameez*. Once in a more comfortable reclining position, she allowed her hand to rest on her growing belly. She was pregnant again, and the thought of putting anything down her throat threw her excitable nausea into overdrive.

Fatima shrugged, plucked a large slice from the plate, and sank her teeth into its juicy flesh. Her gold bangles clinked in harmony with the tapping of her bare foot against the cool tiles. Together they watched their children play in front of them. Safwat, rolling an unpainted wooden truck across the floor with his *vroom-vroom* sounds, was growing into a strong little boy. The vast baby fat of his infancy was almost entirely gone as he approached his third year. He had his father's great auburn eyes and the unruly, wavy hair of his mother, cropped close to his head and forcefully combed with a center part, doing its best to accentuate a pair of oversized ears. His skin was a light wheatish brown, its fairness the combined result of his mother's luminous complexion and her insistence that they stay sheltered from the sun, lest it sully their fine coloring. Iqra also shared the natural skin tone of her aunt, mother, and cousin, but had grown darker through her refusal to stay off the rooftop terrace, allowing the sun to color her skin into a shade of rich milky chai.

Safwat walked across the white tiled floors in his bare feet to his aunt Fatima and reached for the plate of mangoes.

"Auntie, please?" he asked, smiling up to reveal a mouth full of uncommonly straight teeth.

"Yes, *meri jaanu*," Fatima said, pressing her lips to Safwat's forehead and then handing him the plumpest slice of fruit from the plate.

Ammi smiled to herself, witnessing the exchange between her sister and son. *Alhamdulillah, all praise and thanks to Allah*, she was blessed with a wonderful, loving family. Her gaze drifted over to Iqra, playing with a golden-haired doll a British client of Imran's had brought as a gift. She hummed softly as she braided the doll's hair.

"What's her name?" Ammi asked her niece, prompting the small girl to look up, brows furrowed at the interruption.

"Cinderella," Iqra answered, turning back to the doll's yellow mane.

Confused at first, Ammi quickly recalled an animated movie that had been playing in Lahore's British cinema. Never one to deny his daughter an experience, Imran had taken Iqra to a screening when it was first released several weeks before. Prior to seeing the movie, Iqra had named her doll Amina but changed it immediately at her first glimpse of the life-like cartoon-blond princess. Since the movie's debut, she had become inseparable from her toy, tucking it away into the pockets of her colorful *salwar kameez* suits and sleeping with it at night. She had also renamed the family's pet parakeet, kept in an ornate, heavy brass birdcage, Gus. The film was cut off abruptly at the end just before Cinderella and her new husband, a *gora* prince, were said to kiss. Nothing could be done to conceal the cartoon Cinderella's bare legs, arms, and neck, a detail that didn't escape Ammi and prevented Safwat from seeing the film, not that he had shown any interest in it. Iqra's doll had been dressed in more modest attire: long *abayas* hand stitched by their maid to match several of Iqra's own suits.

"Amina was a beautiful name, *mashaAllah*." Ammi countered, "She should keep it."

Iqra sighed defiantly. "Cinderella."

"She looks funny!" Safwat squealed, pointing a finger sticky with mango juice at Iqra's beloved doll.

Iqra glared back and scrambled to her feet, her long braid swinging around with the abrupt jerking of her skinny body. "You look funny," she mumbled, "Cinderella looks perfect." Gently stroking Cinderella's flaxen hair with her tiny hand, she brought the doll's plastic ear to her lips, whispered a secret, and made her exit through a heavy sandalwood door that led to the rooftop terrace.

Nazar was born at home at the onset of the monsoon season during a power outage. Where Safwat had slipped from his mother with speed and relative gentility, Nazar took his time and made sure she knew he was going to do as he pleased, when he pleased. When he finally emerged after thirty-two hours of intense labor, his lungs wasted no time in piercing the humid air with constant screams for attention.

Abbu whispered the first words a baby should hear into his son's right ear to ward off Shayton, "God is great. There is no God but Allah. Muhammed is the messenger of Allah. Come to prayer."

Seven days after the birth and following the shaving of Nazar's head and circumcision, the midwife, a dais from the neighboring family, suggested Ammi choose another name as "the one who gives" wasn't suitable for a boy who demanded so much from everyone around him. The name was kept in the misguided hope that he would grow into it. A sheep was slaughtered in the courtyard and its meat distributed to the local poor who waited eagerly at the gate with outstretched arms for their alms.

Safwat fell instantly in love with his colicky younger brother. He grew so accustomed to Nazar's wailing that he would rest his hand over his brother's chest while he slept, just to make sure he was still breathing.

"You will wake him up, and we will never sleep," Ammi would whisper to Safwat, taking his hand into hers. The two would stare down together into the cot as Nazar rested, the sweetness of his slumber giving a momentary respite from the intensity of his waking hours.

Iqra was less interested in her new cousin and had begun school. Her mornings were filled with daily Quran classes by a tutor who came to the house. Shortly after, she was whisked away in a rickshaw to a private all-girls academy for a secular, English education. She was an astute student who, even at such a young age, was quick to grasp all manner of learning she was provided. At school, she excelled and made friends with both the Pakistani girls from similarly affluent backgrounds and the white-skinned daughters of British expatriates.

Safwat spent his days at home with the women of the household and his brother Nazar. Abbu left for work every morning after praying Fajr and came home long after Safwat was asleep. His time with his father was limited to Friday afternoons, when he would return home to collect his son for Jummah, praying at the masjid together.

The maid had an eight-year-old son named Aadil. He visited twice a week and taught Safwat to play cricket and catch the green, long-legged Lynx spiders in the shrubs of their courtyard. Despite being the son of a servant, an untouchable, Aadil grew close to Safwat by virtue of being sole playmates. The boys envied each other's situations. In his naiveté, Safwat saw nothing beyond a boy who could come and go as he pleased, riding his faded blue bicycle with the wobbly wheels outside the safe confines of their gated house and onto the lively streets of Lahore. Aadil saw a boy who had every privilege he would never have, in a caste he could never be a part of, who was so sheltered that he would never comprehend the difficulties everyone outside the gate was forced to confront. Aadil frequently rode into the courtyard with his pockets full of stolen mangoes or a fresh grapefruit on his lap.

"I got a treat today!" Aadil shouted, throwing a leg clad in a dirty brown *salwar* over the banana seat and hopping off his bike. He walked over to Safwat and dropped a plump, barely ripened grapefruit on the sandstone.

Delighted by the gifts, Safwat always accepted them with an excited smile. He picked up the golden fruit and squeezed it between his fingers.

"It's got a spot on it," Safwat said frowning, turning the fruit over in his hands and pointing at a single blemish, "right here."

Aadil took the grapefruit from Safwat and peeled the flesh open, its fragrant juice dripping down his slender arm. "Look here. It's perfect inside."

Safwat reached up greedily and retrieved the grapefruit from Aadil. Splitting its juicy meat in half, he handed a portion to his friend.

It was impossible for Safwat to grasp the risk Aadil took picking them from a private tree, a danger Safwat would never be exposed to because he could afford to buy all the fruit he wanted. Safwat had never experienced hunger that couldn't be satiated immediately, where Aadil had spent countless nights in his bed with a rumbling stomach.

From the veranda of the second floor where she was watching the exchange, Ammi's voice carried down to the boys outside.

"Come in for lunch."

As they made their way in, Aadil's mother gently slapped his leg with her handmade straw broom and motioned him to the right, where his small lunch of *dal* and rice sat waiting on a plastic plate designated for servants. Safwat wiped his fingers, still dripping with bits of pulp and grapefruit juice, across his knee-length gray *kameez* shirt and made his way upstairs. A white sheet was sprawled on the living room floor and topped with fine, gold-rimmed bone chinaware and copper *balti* dishes containing fragrant *dal*, steaming lamb *biryani*, *seekh* kababs, golden fried *samosas*, and Safwat's favorite, *gosht karahi*—tender, succulent mutton pieces in a spicy tomato gravy—and *naan*.

The women arranged themselves on the sheet, Ammi using her fingers to assemble large portions of food onto Safwat's plate. They ate in silence, Safwat soon forgetting his friend downstairs and the meager portions of Aadil's own bowl.

Chapter
2

Eid al-Adha, the feast of sacrifice, was always a
magnificent occasion to the family and to all Muslims
worldwide. The celebrations were planned weeks in
advance with preparations for feasting and festivities
running long into the night. Members of the extended
family and friends trickled through the house during
three days of commemoration, in honor of Abraham's
willingness to sacrifice his son on command from Allah.
Passing this test, his son Ishmael was spared by Allah
and replaced by a ram.

Abbu had spent the morning reciting the event as it was recorded in the Quran, with Safwat reading along from the holy text. Safwat had sat in disbelief that Abbu knew it by heart.

Abbu, with his eyes closed, recited softly, "Abraham prayed: My Lord, grant me a doer of good deeds. So we gave him the good news of a forbearing son. But when he became of age to work with him, he said: O my son, I have seen in a dream that I should sacrifice you; so consider what is your view. He said: O my father, do as you are commanded; if Allah please you will find me patient. So when they had both submitted, and he had thrown him down upon his forehead, and we called out to him saying, O Abraham, you have indeed fulfilled the vision. Thus do we reward the doers of good. Surely this is a manifest trial. And we ransomed him with a great sacrifice."

Safwat's mind wandered from the passage as Abbu continued with his recitation. He wondered if Abbu would be willing to sacrifice him if Allah tested him in such a way. Peering up at his father, he hoped if it ever happened Allah would ask for Nazar, who was a naughty boy, and not him.

In the next room, Ammi stood before her full-length mirror dressed in an intricately beaded maroon *anarkali* suit. She was almost ready to give birth to Abbu's third child and had prayed zealously for a little girl. She had decided to try and put an end to the unpleasant task of monkey business when she finally had a daughter. As much as she enjoyed his general company, coupling with her husband was a chore she could live without. Once she had produced two sons and a daughter, there would be no further need for her husband to rut on top of her.

Inspecting herself in the mirror, she turned sideways to view her bulky belly and then wrapped her long black plait under an opaque *dupatta*, concealing it completely.

Walking over to the door of an oversized armoire, she slipped her fingers under the thick sandalwood and pulled it open. Hanging neatly among an expanse of her own jeweled, vibrantly colored dresses were Safwat's and Nazar's new *salwar kameezes*, freshly pressed by the maid. She plucked the hangers from the rod and inspected them.

They will look so handsome in these, mashaAllah, she thought and slid the back of her hand down the crisp linen. Her thoughts were interrupted by the bleating of a goat, and she sauntered slowly to the window to take in the animals below.

Five goats, decorated with bells and colorful ribbons, stood roped in the courtyard waiting to make the required sacrifice to honor Abraham's. It had been years since the surrender of animals had bothered Ammi, but having children of her own had rekindled the sadness she felt at their loss. Just as she had in her youth, the children always named and played with the goats until the moment of sacrifice came. Since the purpose of the sacrifice was to give up something you had grown to care for, what transpired between her children and the animals was exactly what was supposed to. Unfortunately, the knowledge of this did little to lessen the effects her children's emotional outcries had on her heart. It was years before her mother had revealed to her that a third of the animals sacrificed by her father ended up on her own plate.

An *adhaan* cried out in the distance, and she knew it was time to go for Eid prayers.

Together with Fatima, Imran, and Iqra, the family made their way out the front door to the rickshaws waiting outside.

Iqra positioned herself between her aunt and mother, smiling up in excitement for the day ahead.

"Are you wearing a fragrance, Iqra?" Fatima asked, scrunching her nose and then leaning into her daughter to take a deeper sniff.

"It's just an attar of roses and musk," Iqra replied, twisting slightly from her position between Ammi and Fatima, and leaning into her aunt. "It's Auntie's."

Ammi glanced toward Fatima with a pleading look of apology. "I told her she could use it when she wanted, but I didn't think it would be worn outside the house."

The fragrance wafted through the rickshaw, its warm scent of Gallica roses, precious cedar wood, and heady deer musk permeating the small space.

"A little less next time, *jaanu*," Fatima conceded, a smile spreading across her face, "but it does smell lovely."

Iqra had started to blossom into a striking young lady. Her monthly bleeding had commenced the year before, and in a few short months, her facial features and body began the rapid transition from girl to woman. Her long black hair was kept under a gracefully swept white headscarf and gold floral brooch, which only improved the startling amber and gold of her large, heavily lashed eyes. Her uncommonly slender aquiline nose, frequently admired by the girls at school, Asian and *gori* alike, was much enhanced by a pronounced set of cheekbones. The attention she attracted did not go unnoticed by her or her parents, and she reveled in it privately. Far too young for marriage, she was still old enough to inquire about. Questions regarding her availability as a potential future bride for their sons came to Imran through friends in the same social circle, each one systematically rejected in favor of his nephew, Safwat. Iqra was a dutiful daughter, helping her mother with the management of the household and learning to cook when time permitted from a second maid the family had installed in the home. Most of her time was spent engrossed in her studies, where she favored geography and social sciences, learning about places she would never see.

They approached The Badshahi Mosque, and all let out a collective gasp as the driver turned into the mass of foot traffic crowding the street. The Badshashi was a masterpiece of architecture, and Ammi always marveled in its extravagance when she was permitted to visit it. Migrants from the northeast who had lost their glittering Taj Mahal to India in the partition reluctantly acknowledged Badshahi to be more ornate and certainly much larger. If picked up and moved, the entire Taj Mahal would fit into Badshahi's courtyard. Four soaring minarets that appeared to reach up and touch the sky framed the grandeur of its sandstone courtyard and exquisitely detailed façade of stone carving and marble inlays. For Eid prayers, Badshahi welcomed 150,000 worshippers, all traipsing across its marble and tile to prostrate themselves in uniform subjugation to Allah. It was a glorious spectacle that moved many to tears.

Making their way to the women's section, Ammi, Fatima, and Iqra laid their rugs eastward and soon became engrossed in the recitation of the Quran and *rakats*. The beauty of the *surrahs* persuaded the movement of their bodies in all positions of the *salah*. Their bodies, hearts, and minds became one with the prayer. At least that was how it felt to Ammi.

During the second *rakat*, when Ammi was bending forward, a gush of water was released from her womb. It ran swiftly down her leg and splashed onto her prayer mat.

"It's a boy!" shouted the dais, wiping her bloodied hands on a scrap of linen. Then she handed Ammi's son to Fatima for cleaning.

There was no time for the midwife or Fatima to rejoice in the live birth, which had left Ammi listless and hemorrhaging in her bed. Her son had been slow to come, and when he was stuck in the birth canal with just a tiny hand making its way out, the dais had to turn him as best she could before using curved high forceps to pull him from Ammi's weak body. The newest addition to the Miah family entered the world amidst a rush of blood and the agonizing screams of his mother.

"*As'alullaahal-'Adheema Rabbal-'Arshil-'Adheemi 'an yashfiyaka*," the dais prayed desperately as she attempted to stop Ammi's hemorrhaging, coaxing her uterus back into place. *I ask Almighty Allah, Lord of the Magnificent Throne, to make you well.*

Ammi let out a soft groan. She was too weak from the loss of blood and the exertion of energy to do anything but yield to her body's primal response to the pain, whimpering.

"*As'alullaahal-'Adheema Rabbal-'Arshil-'Adheemi 'an yashfiyaka*," the dais repeated five more times, massaging Ammi's belly. The soothing movement of skilled hands on her flesh relaxed and comforted Ammi back into silence.

Slowly, the flow of blood began to lighten, and the dais was able to apply a black salve to the lacerations caused by the violent delivery. "*As'alullaahal-'Adheema Rabbal-'Arshil-'Adheemi 'an yashfiyaka.*"

Fatima reentered the room with a mound of embroidered bright plum and crimson Kashmiri patoo blankets. Gently lifting Ammi's knees, she placed several under her legs and elevated them. She moved to the side of the heavy ebony baroque bed and spread a final patoo over the length of Ammi's body. Her breath was ragged, and Fatima stretched her arm out to press her hand lightly against Ammi's cheek.

"She's on fire," Fatima said quietly, and looked to the dais.

"*Alhamdulillah* the bleeding has stopped," the elderly woman replied. "It will be a few days, but *inshaAllah* she should be well enough in a short time."

Relief washed over Fatima. She turned back to her sister. "Will this will be her last child?" she asked quietly.

The dais set down her clay pot of black salve, lifted a ceramic pitcher from the dressing table, and dispensed a stream of water over her aged hands and into the bowl below.

"This was a difficult birth, yes," she conceded, "but not as damaging as your own." She dried her hands on a clean cloth of linen and turned her attention back to Fatima. "She will be physically capable of having more sons, yes. Whether or not she is willing to repeat a birth like this...for now, the answer is between herself and Allah until she is able to say so herself."

"She wanted a daughter," Fatima replied in a light tone.

"Allah has kept her strong and blessed her with three healthy sons," the dais responded matter-of-factly. "Daughters will come by marriage, if not of her own body, *inshaAllah*. And Allah always knows best."

"*Alhamdulillah* for everything," Fatima whispered.

Chapter
3

In January of 1966, nineteen years into
Pakistan's independence, Pakistan and India finally
signed an agreement to end the hostilities that had
plagued both nations since the Indo-Pakistani war of
1965. With the Tashkent Declaration, India relinquished
occupied boundaries, but the climate of Lahore was still
one of discontentment. It had been widely believed that
Pakistan was on the verge of winning the war. Whether
this belief was legitimate or the result of media
propaganda, no one had any verifiable facts. What was
known, however, was that the signing of the declaration

by President Muhammad Ayub Khan threw him and his party into a political tailspin. He was forced into seclusion, his power undermined by demonstrations and rioting throughout the country. This led to the birth of the Pakistan People's Party and the start of a meteoric rise in popularity for Zulfikar Ali Bhutto, one of Khan's dismissed ministers.

With a wedding for Safwat and Iqra to plan, Ammi had little interest in what was taking place on the city streets with the exception of how unscheduled, pop-up political marches might disrupt her preparations. This wedding had to be a lavish, traditional series of celebrations with festivities spanning over five days. The entire household was abuzz.

The necessity of the nuptials couldn't have been more urgent in Ammi's opinion. Safwat, at age nineteen, had completed his finance degree at the Government College of Lahore and was about to begin his accountancy career in the offices of his uncle's packaging plant. Fueled by western demand for inexpensive labor and cheap boxes, the plant was now exporting massive quantities of its product overseas to Europe and America. The family coffers flourished, and the wedding was intended to showcase not only their wealth, but the alliance of the household, strengthened through the marriage of the cousins.

Ammi also knew her firstborn was in desperate need of a wife for other reasons, having discovered him in the kitchen the day before the announcement with his *lora* in the mouth of Eliza, a poor housemaid they had recently added to their staff. Ammi stood horrified while Safwat scrambled to pull his *salwar* pants back up to their rightful position around his waist, and the pretty young maid began to cry, begging not to be thrown back out on the street.

Zina, the stringent Islamic edict governing unlawful and immoral sexual relations between the unmarried, was the last thing she had ever expected to encounter in her own kitchen. Picking up a heavy, long walnut *doi* from beside the sink, she raced toward her son with an animalistic growl and proceeded to slap the wooden spoon against his arms and chest. Eliza cowered in the corner, her sobs turning into howling when Basha, the trusted senior housemaid, Aadil's mother, entered the room from the adjoining garden after hearing the commotion.

Standing slack jawed, Basha didn't dare intervene in the onslaught of aggression that her *sahiba* levied against her son, who remained still, accepting his mother's punishment in complete submission.

The *doi* dropped to the floor tiles with a weighty thud, and Ammi soon followed, collapsing to her knees in despair.

"How dare you!" she wailed at her son before turning her attention to the bawling Eliza. "Get this *doe dolla raande* out of my house!"

The young maid let out another howl. "I'm no two-dollar whore," she proclaimed between sobs. "He promised to take me as a second wife!"

Ammi gasped, exhaled, and released another anguished cry

"Did you make this ridiculous promise to a servant?" Ammi looked up at her son, who was quick to avert his eyes. He shifted from one foot to the other, fumbling with the string of his *salwar*. "You could destroy everything we have built here—your marriage to my own sister's daughter—our beloved Iqra, to bed a sewer rat? To take a *nokarni* as a second wife? You haven't even claimed your first wife, and already you are making plans for a second? With a street urchin?"

"I wasn't really going to…" Safwat started, interrupted by a despondent cry from Eliza.

"You weren't really going to what?" Ammi countered. "You weren't really going to marry a girl you were so hasty to sully? Is this what we've raised? A man of such character?"

"No…I meant…" he started again, backpedaling. "I can have another wife! I can have any woman who pleases me as long as there is a *nikkah*! It's my right!"

"Your right ends when it is your uncle's money that pays your salary! Pays your father's salary," she screamed. "Your right ends when you are married to his daughter, the Iqra of all our hearts! Or do you wish this marriage to not take place and dishonor us all?"

"I want to marry Iqra," he cried. "Who wouldn't want Iqra?"

She imagined his mind wandering to his beautiful cousin. There was nobody in this city who could hold a candle to her magnificence. Aside from being striking to the eye, she was spectacularly brilliant. Iqra had been educated alongside him, obtaining a Bachelor's of Science in physical geography when women rarely completed secondary school. Her mastery of the English language was so great that her father had begun asking her to sit in on boardroom meetings and teleconferences with western clients. Ammi knew Safwat was looking forward to nothing in his future as much as making Iqra his bride. He appeared shamed by what he had risked.

"I'm sorry Ammi," he puffed out in what seemed to be genuine regret. "I'm so sorry."

Ammi rose from her position on the floor and brushed her hands down the front of her lavender *kameez* suit. She raised a shaking hand to her forehead, patting her disheveled hair and tucked a loose strand behind her ear.

Composing herself, she said, "It is out of the question, in any event. We do not take more than one wife in this family. Iqra and her parents would not tolerate bringing such shame to their household, a son-in-law making a mockery of their daughter's standing with any second wife, let alone a servant."

The maid gasped, and Ammi turned to her.

"You will be given a gold necklace set of almost 75 grams, worth more than you could earn in a lifetime of scrubbing floors, and you will be gone from this house without a word of complaint this afternoon."

Eliza bobbed her head in agreement and scurried through the garden door. She had not given her virtue, only her mouth, and only once. In a city where adulterers could be stoned to death, the set was enormous recompense, and she was grateful for it despite her momentary embarrassment. The sale of the set would pull her family from the slums, a home constructed of particle board and tarp, and leave her with a suitable dowry that could fetch a husband with a comfortable job, a man with a small shop, or perhaps even a handsome footman from a hotel.

Ammi made her way out of the kitchen and retreated to her bedroom to collect the promised gold from its vault. Followed by Basha, she sat down at her writing table to pen a note clarifying that the jewelry was a gift, lest the girl be arrested on question of theft, and the whole incident be brought to life again.

The dates of the wedding festivities were set by Ammi and Fatima, who had no knowledge of the earlier events, for the following day. The proposal party, which had been assembled with some haste, took place in the afternoon. It was a formality, the first of the extensive string of traditional wedding celebrations that generally involved the elders in the family. As the elders were no longer alive, the party itself consisted of the immediate household members.

Iqra sat on the flamboyant, gold-encrusted burgundy sofa in the family's parlor, dressed in a silk and chiffon *anarkali* dress of pale pink. Her mother and Ammi placed themselves on each side, and both took one of her delicate hands into their own. Emerging from the adjoining room, Imran, Abbu, and Safwat stood before Iqra.

"We ask for your blessed daughter's hand in marriage for our son, Safwat, *inshaAllah*," Abbu said, placing his hand on his son's shoulder and turning toward Imran.

Imran looked to his wife and daughter, who dutifully nodded yes. There was no other answer to give. Iqra had looked forward to this day, as all young Punjabi girls did, to fulfill her destiny and complete half of her Islamic deen.

"We accept the marriage proposal of your son and wish them both happy, *inshaAllah*," Imran replied. He turned to Safwat and placed a gold band around the fourth finger of his left hand.

Following suit, Ammi lifted Iqra's hand and gently slid a smaller gold band over the same finger. Iqra smiled to her aunt, who raised her niece's hand to her lips and gently kissed the ring. Fatima stood from her place next to Iqra and motioned to Safwat, who sat down beside his beautiful fiancé. The two did not meet each other's eyes, instead looking respectfully at their own hands as Abbu removed the Holy Quran from its emerald green felt sheath and held the sacred text over the heads of the engaged.

"Bismillah Ar-Rahman Ar-Raheem, Al-hamdu lillahi Rabb il-'alamin, Ar-Rahman Ar-Raheem

Maliki yawmi-d-Din, Iyya-ka na'budu wa iyya-ka nasta'in, Ihdina-sirat al-mustaqim, Sirat al ladhina an'amta 'alai-him, Ghair il-Maghdubi 'alai-him wa la-d-dallin," Abbu recited the Surah Al-Fatihah in a clear and firm voice.

In the name of Allah, the Most Beneficent, the Most Merciful. Praise be to Allah, Lord of the Worlds: The Most Beneficent, the Most Merciful: Owner of the Day of Judgment. Thee alone we worship; Thee alone was ask for help. Show us the straight path: The path of those whom Thou hast favored; Not the path of those who earn Thine anger nor of those who go astray.

With a clap of her hands, Ammi called in Basha, who entered the room carrying a silver tray of tea and spiced *atta* biscuits. Iqra and Safwat were formally engaged.

The next segment of wedding festivities was just with female relatives, so the men of the house were left to their own devices. Lut, who was only nine years old, had been permitted to stay but decided against it in favor of a night of revelry with his older brothers, uncle, and father. Safwat and the men would be hosted by a distant cousin for their own party, the Tael, where the groom's hair would be oiled, and they would feast on sweets and laughter for the evening. Safwat, no longer allowed to see his fiancé until the wedding day, would remain at their cousins' house accompanied by fourteen-year-old Nazar.

For the women, it was the night of the Dholki and Mayoon party, which were combined with the Mehndi celebration, when women crowded into the house to sing, dance, and paint the bride's hands and feet with intricate henna patterns. It was customary to have the three parties separately, but the political climate in Lahore had necessitated combining the events so extended family making the journey even across the city could do so easily without concern for street demonstrations and other, more dangerous scenarios.

Iqra was magnificent in a lawn dress of lemon yellow, trimmed with a pattern of gold and woven lightly with powder blue thread. Her face was devoid of make-up and a matching yellow ribbon ran intertwined through the length of her long, simple braid. Her mother and aunt had brought her into the living room ceremony under the canopy of a canary-hued beaded *dupatta*. She was immediately surrounded by a flock of married women, one who was particularly skilled at the art of henna designs meant to symbolize good luck and longevity to the bride's married life.

Fatima and Ammi walked her to the sofa, which had been festively draped in saffron silk and strings of yellow marigolds. Picking up a diamond-shaped coconut *barfi* coated in a thin layer of edible gold metallic leaf, Ammi brought the treat to Iqra's lips to feed her niece.

"You look beautiful, *mashaAllah*," Ammi whispered.

Iqra beamed as she took a small nibble of the sweet offering.

"Thank you," Iqra replied. "I cannot believe this is all for me."

She pointed toward a young woman positioning herself beside the cylinder *dholki*, her hand beginning to tap the oversized drum. The women in the room, all dressed in various shades of yellow, began to clap and sing in unison, dipping into the trays overflowing with bite-sized sugared delicacies.

Iqra's hands and feet were intricately decorated by the masterful hands of the henna artist. Detailed red *mehndi* in floral and mosaic designs were woven carefully and left to dry. After Iqra's was complete, the artist applied the technique to the fingers and toes of Fatima, Ammi, and the other women at the party. The deep color intensified ten hours later when it was rinsed off, and reached its richest tone just in time for the Baraat, Nikkah, and Rukhsati ceremonies two days later.

For the *baraat*—the entourage the groom brings on his wedding day—Safwat returned to the family home resplendently dressed in an ivory *sherwani* threaded with gold, complete with a turban and *khussay*. Garlands of freshly cut flowers hung around his neck, and he himself sat atop a gleaming white horse, surrounded by Ammi, Abbu, his brothers, and a handful of friends. Aadil had replaced the aging gatekeeper a few years beforehand and taken up the post, but on this day, he walked beside his childhood friend as a member of Safwat's *baraati*.

Once Safwat and the *baraatis* settled down in the main entry of the house, the *nikkah* ceremony officially began. Tucked away in the living room upstairs, Iqra, her parents, and a bridal party of her friends and family sat listening to the commotion below. Every hair on Iqra's body stood on end in anticipation for what was to come.

"This is it, *inshaAllah*," Fatima whispered to her daughter.

Iqra dazzled in all her finery—heavy bangles and rings of solid gold, matching chandelier earrings, and her *nath*, a hooped nose ring that attached with a hair-thin chain to a cuff on her ear. A gold *tikka* encrusted with rubies dangled over her forehead, and an identical *jhumar* rested at her temple. Her gown was of the deepest, purest red that could be found, and its beading of minuscule gold droplets and flecks of crystal were so fine that it shimmered like a thousand prisms across the walls.

The Imam entered the room and confirmed that a proposal by Safwat for marriage had been made, an *Ijab-e-Qubul*, and stated the sum of the *mahr* – the amount of money promised to her.

"Do you accept this proposal?" he asked.

"She accepts," Imran replied.

The Imam turned to Iqra and repeated the question three times, to which Iqra answered yes to each. A large document was placed before her to sign along with her father and a distant male cousin. Her hand shook nervously as she made her mark. Butterflies fluttered in her stomach.

"*Barak Allah hu laka wa baa rak Allah hu alaika wa jama'aa bainakuma fi khair*," the Imam said.

Allah bless you and shower his blessings on you, and place goodness between both of you.

The Imam returned to the entry and informed the Safwat that Iqra had accepted his proposal, including the *mahr* amount.

"Do you accept Iqra, daughter of Imran Miah, as your wife?" he asked.

"*Qabool hai*," Safwat replied. *I accept.*

The question was asked and answered again three times before the same document was presented to Safwat, his father, and his brother Nazar to sign.

"*Barak Allah hu laka wa baa rak Allah hu alaika wa jama'aa bainakuma fi khair,*" the Imam repeated the dua again, as he had upstairs.

Allah bless you and shower his blessings on you, and place goodness between both of you.

The *baraati* erupted with applause and cheering, at which point Iqra presented herself with her party at the top of the spiral staircase. A collective gasp rang out below as she proceeded down the steps, regal in her finery.

Safwat took her fingers into his hands as she reached the bottom of the stairs.

"*Wallahi,*" he swore to Allah, "I have never in my life seen, or even heard of, a more beautiful woman than you are today, *mashaAllah.*"

Iqra blushed under the heavy makeup and lowered her eyes. "Thank you, Safwat." She said to her cousin. Her husband.

Imran and Fatima embraced their daughter tightly. Fatima's eyes welled up with tears, and she leaned in for a final whisper in her daughter's ear.

"Do not be afraid for this night," she reassured her again. "It does not hurt for more than a moment."

Iqra nodded her head yes, grateful for the advice her mother had given her. It was counsel that most young, virginal brides were denied. Discussing the wedding night was rarely ever done, even between mother and daughter, beyond a basic parable that frequently involved an eel and a cave. Fatima had broken with the propriety of custom many nights beforehand and given a far more graphic description to Iqra of what she could expect.

With the Holy Quran held over her head to demonstrate a bestowment of blessings upon her, the bride was led out of the great hall by Safwat and the *baraat*. Iqra stepped inside the luxury town car outside, decorated with strings of flowers and waiting to take the new bride and groom to their honeymoon suite at the five star Avari Hotel.

Chapter
4

Late the following morning, Ammi rose from
her bed. The events of the night had left her with a
blinding headache. Abbu had seen Nazar and Lut off to
school, their protests at taking a day off after their
brother's wedding celebrations falling on deaf ears. She
wrapped herself in a simple orange *dupatta* from the
wardrobe and splashed cold water from a basin across
her face. Abbu walked in, a crumpled newspaper in his
hand and a smile.

"We need to get Safwat and Iqra from the hotel
and bring them home," he said.

"Just a cup of chai first," Ammi replied. She needed the caffeine and a bit of hot liquid to help her wake up and soothe her aching head.

At the jingle of Ammi's bell, Basha entered their dark chamber. She set a hot cup of tea on the dresser and drew the curtains, allowing a stream of light to fall across the room. It was nearly eleven o'clock. Ammi had an hour before the couple expected them for lunch at the hotel and to be brought back home.

She took a sip from the gold-rimmed porcelain cup. "I'll be down in forty-five minutes." It was Abbu's cue to leave, and after twenty years of marriage, she knew that he wouldn't stay when she was in no mood for company.

Once her teacup was empty, and she had been attired in an elegant white and sapphire blue beaded *salwar kameez*, she and Abbu made their way to the Avari to meet Iqra and Safwat in the hotel's restaurant.

"*Assalamualeikum*," she greeted her son and new daughter. Both leaned in to kiss her and Abbu on each cheek.

"*Waleikumsalam*," they replied almost in unison.

Once seated at a table, Iqra avoided eye contact with the aunt and uncle who had always been like parents to her. She carefully picked up a crystal goblet filled with lychee juice and took a small sip. "Did the celebrations go on for much longer after we left?"

Ammi smiled and reached her hand across the table, taking Iqra's into her own. "How can a wedding party continue without the bride and groom?"

She knew Iqra would share the same shyness she had had so many years before, seeing her husband's parents after the wedding night. Her mind wandered for a moment to an evening less than a year before the partition, one where she was the bride. She hadn't been afforded the privacy of a five-star hotel. Instead, she laid for the first time with Abbu, mortified in the knowledge that beyond the door of their small room everyone in the house knew what they were doing. Her own mother had warned her only moments before to remove the expensive wedding garment she wore, lest she spill her blood or Abbu's seed on it. It wasn't until the act was complete that she understood why, or what any of it even was or meant. The next morning she was too ashamed to make eye contact with her aunt, her new mother-in-law.

She shook the memory away. "Did you have breakfast?"

"No, Ammi." Safwat nodded and smiled toward Iqra.

Her face flushed crimson. "We had tea and biscuits. The suite had a kettle and lovely snacks. Thank you for the basket, Ammi."

Ammi had arranged for the hotel to prepare the room with a hamper full of Iqra's and Safwat's favorite treats. Her heart warmed at being called Ammi instead of Auntie, but she knew there would be confusion in the house with both she and Fatima sharing the honorable title.

"I love hearing Ammi on your lips, Iqra *jaanu*. It is what I have been waiting for since you were promised to Safwat. But perhaps, for now, out of respect for my sister, I might forego the honor, and you may continue to call me Auntie."

Iqra relaxed in her chair and met Ammi's eyes for the first time since they sat down together. "I thought about that for some time, but would prefer to call you Ammi. I will call my mother Amma, as I have done for a while now."

Ammi scooped up a thick piece of curried potato with a flaky bit of *paratha*. Her heart swelled inside her chest. "I am so glad to hear that, my sweet girl."

They finished their lunch at a relaxed pace and made their way home two hours later than they had expected. The traffic leading to their front gate was unusually heavy, and the driver was in no particular hurry to find an alternate route. Ammi turned her eyes to the crowds surrounding the busy road. It wasn't unusual to see the sidewalks bustling, but the commotion that afternoon wasn't the typical stream of pedestrians coming and going down the thoroughfare. People stood talking, while others attempted to catch a glimpse of something farther down the street.

"Is there an accident?" she asked the driver.

He rolled down his window as a police officer approached the vehicle, and words were exchanged in hushed voices too low for Ammi to understand. The officer looked nervously toward the passengers in the back and raised his hand to motion their car through. As the crowd split and cars pulled to the side to make way, Ammi realized the blockade had been established right in front of their own home.

Panic rose in her chest and she shook the back of her driver's seat. "Tell me now what is going on!"

"I do not know, *Sahiba*."

Men in their khaki military jumpsuits and green berets lined the street, and as they approached the gate, one waved the car in. Aadil was nowhere in sight.

The family all burst from the car. Ammi's approach to the front door was halted by an officer who asked to speak with Abbu and Safwat. Iqra and Ammi were left to the side to wait out their rising panic, both screaming toward the house for Fatima and Imran to show themselves.

They came, but not in the way the women had wished. Two stretchers with bloodied white sheets did little to conceal the form of bodies that emerged. A hand with Imran's white-gold watch and a swatch of Fatima's pink *kameez* protruded from the slips of fabric covering their lifeless figures.

Ammi released a wail that pierced through the courtyard as she fell to her knees and tugged violently at her hair. Iqra, who had been holding Ammi's arm with a grip that left a trail of indents and bruises, lost all control and fainted onto the sandstone.

It was only after Aadil's statement had been taken from his hospital bed that the gruesome details of the attack were fully revealed. His version of events were the sole firsthand account of what had transpired. They were delayed by hours because of a gunshot wound through the leg that required immediate emergency surgery, making his statement impossible to ascertain beforehand.

"They came down from the roof and into the side courtyard," Basha said. "I was preparing dinner, and three just walked in through the door. Waajida was in the pantry sweeping up the *toor dal* she spilled, and with a gun barrel between my eyes, I was shoved into the pantry with her, and they latched us in. The rest is Aadil's account, which he relayed to the police and then to me."

Ammi let out a whimper, her eyes stinging through hours of tears for her lost sister and cousin. "The police are too corrupt to trust. Tell me what happened."

Abbu sat hunched beside her, giving in to his own emotion and grief, unable to speak.

The old maid's hands trembled and twisted the linen of her dusty *kameez*. "Aadil heard my scream and ran into the house, first to me in the kitchen. I told him men had broken in—men with guns." She choked back her tears. "*Sahiba*, I begged him not to go up. To run and

57

get the police—but he insisted." The weight of this admission was not lost on Ammi, even in her despair. If it had been Safwat, she would've begged the same of her son. She knew it. Just as Safwat would have, Aadil put the people who had cared for him his whole life before his own. Ammi waved at Basha to continue, too deep in her own sorrow to console a maid whose son had been spared from death by will of Allah.

"He ran upstairs to *Mem Sahiba* when she screamed, and I sent Waajida to fetch the police. They knew there was jewelry from the wedding last night. They wanted the jewelry."

Ammi played the scene in her mind. The blood-curdling scream of her sister as men barged into her room. The younger maid running out to the police station. Aadil racing up the stairs. Her stomach lurched, and she forced aside the pressing need to vomit.

"Aadil said *Mem Sahiba* was begging Imran Ji to give the jewelry to them. He refused, and they attacked him, two of them, throwing their fists into his face. Aadil went in to pull them off Imran Ji, and that's when the first gun went off. That's when they shot Aadil in the leg."

She lifted her hands to her mouth to smother a groan. Her head shook back and forth. "Then they shot *Mem Sahiba* and Imran Ji both and ran!"

The sickness in Ammi's throat forced its way through the little self-control she had left and spilled onto the marble floor. Abbu put his hand gently on her shoulder, and she flung herself up and walked down the long corridor. She entered a small study where Imran had concealed a safe behind a heavy mahogany chair, and pulled the boxes of jewels out from their steel cage. With a shriek, she threw the contents of the boxes over the banister, where they crashed in a thousand directions, spilling onto the floor below.

Whatever they had been worth had no value to her against the lives of the two people—her sister, Abbu's brother—who had offered a safe haven and a future in their home when Ammi and Abbu were forced to flee from theirs all those many years ago. Those jewels were covered in the blood of her beloved kin.

The Cracked Pot

An Indian water bearer had two large pots, each hanging on an end of a pole and carried across the back of his neck. One pot was perfect, always delivering the full portion of water at the end of the long walk from the well to his master's house. One pot was cracked, always arriving only half full.

For a full two years this went on daily, the bearer delivering only one and a half pots of water to the house. The perfect pot was proud of its accomplishments, faultless to the end for which it was made. The poor cracked pot was ashamed of its imperfection, miserable that it wasn't able to carry out the job for which it was created. After two years of bitter failure, it spoke to the water bearer one day by the well.

"I am ashamed of myself, and I want to apologize to you."

"Why?" asked the bearer. "What are you ashamed of?"

"I have been able, for these past two years, to deliver only half my load because this crack in my side causes water to leak out all the way back to your master's house. Because of my flaws, you have to do all of this work, and you don't get a full reward for your efforts." the pot said.

The water bearer felt sorry for the cracked pot, and in his compassion said, "As we return to the master's house, look along your side of the path."

On the trip back, the old cracked pot did as the bearer said, taking notice of the sun warming the wild flowers on his side of the path, and this lifted his spirits slightly. But at the end of the trail, its melancholy was renewed having again leaked out half its load along the way.

Seeing its sadness once more, the bearer said to the pot, "You noticed the flowers only on your side of your path? I have always known about your flaw, and I took advantage of it. Long ago I planted seeds on your side of the path only, and every day as we walked back from the stream, you've watered them. For two years I have been able to pick these beautiful flowers to decorate my master's table. Without you being just the way you are, he would not have this beauty to grace his house. You and your perceived flaw have provided equally to the perfect pot without a crack."

Carolyn
1978 - San Francisco Bay Area, California

Carolyn was eight months pregnant when Nazar asked her on their first date. She had a history of dating tall, bulky white men and preferred when they came with a head of light hair and a pair of baby blues, just like her own. She was confident, and her friends frequently confirmed, that the father of the child she was carrying matched this description. She couldn't be certain. The night of conception was barely more than a tequila blur, and the guy was gone before she woke up the next morning without leaving so much as a name, a phone number, or even a thank you. What she was certain of now was that this slight man with the funny accent was definitely, definitely not her type. He was cute in his own way, just not in her way.

Nazar and Carolyn had shared a British Literature class at the community college before she had dropped out and he had moved on to graduate from Cal State Hayward. He hadn't given much notice to her leaving until she turned up at his gas station three years later with her bloated belly, asking if there was more Pepsi in the back. He recognized her instantly.

"Carolyn, yeah?" he asked tentatively, placing the cans on the counter.

She picked at a piece of her hair and twirled it loosely around her finger. "Yeah," she replied, knowing that she was eyeing him with a mixture of mild recognition and heightened suspicion.

"Nazar," he said, adding quickly, "We had a class together at Chabot. You probably don't remember..."

"Oh, yeahhhhh." A classroom. She felt herself smile with relief. That was much better than a dark, dodgy nightclub. "I remember you." Her hand moved to her belly, and his eyes followed.

"When did you get married?"

Poor fool had probably heard of American couples running off to Reno and Las Vegas to wed quickly. No doubt he pictured her in a convertible, white veil flapping in the wind as she approached a drive-through chapel.

"Oh, no." She paused and diverted her eyes from his. "I'm not married." She wasn't ashamed, so she didn't understand why the revelation of this detail to him made her feel strangely embarrassed. "Just me and my peanut." She patted her stomach.

He smiled back at her.

"Can I take you out for dinner sometime?" he blurted.

Carolyn couldn't help but laugh, which clearly made Nazar uncomfortable. Realizing he thought she was laughing at him and not the ridiculousness of being asked out by a man when her baby was due in the less than a month, she swiftly apologized. "I'm sorry. I'm not laughing at you. Really, I'm not. I just can't believe you'd want to take me out. I'm as big as a house!"

"Friday at seven?" he asked, unfazed. "It is a safe night to leave the station. Not a glamorous enterprise, I realize, but with help from my father, I was able to purchase it last year, and I care about it."

Carolyn picked up a pen and a scrap of receipt paper from the counter and started to scribble. "Friday at seven it is, then." She slid the paper toward him, pressing it forward slowly with a cherry-colored finger nail, which she suddenly realized looked about as ridiculous and out of place as she did. As she turned and walked out, she paused to watch as Nazar picked up the slip of paper and tucked her address away in his shirt pocket.

Mimi's birth turned out to be the first time in her life that Carolyn was positive she had done something right. One look at the daughter resting in her arms was all it took for everything to make sense in her world. When Nazar walked into the hospital room with flowers soon after, it was the second time in her life she was positive she had done something right.

He handed her a bouquet of white roses and fern. "How are you feeling?"

The cellophane around the blooms crinkled loudly, and both looked over instinctively to make sure Mimi didn't stir from her tiny cot a few feet away.

"Sorry," he said in a hushed whisper.

Carolyn giggled quietly. "Thank you for the flowers. This is the first time anyone ever bought me any." She dipped her face lightly into the perennials and inhaled deeply. The heady scent was relaxing and beautiful.

"How is that possible?" he countered, bewilderment showing on his face.

Carolyn shrugged.

It was possible because she had nobody else in her life. She could hardly classify any of her previous encounters with men as dates, and her young girlfriends had all fizzled off as her pregnancy progressed. For all she knew, her father was still chasing skirts somewhere in Texas. Her mother? Who knew where she was? The last time she had word from the woman was four months prior in a birthday card, postmarked from New Jersey, without a return address. Up until then, Carolyn had assumed she was in Florida, where the card posted the year before had been mailed from.

Nazar was constant. She had only known him for three and a half weeks, but his presence had become so steady that it felt like they had been friends much longer. He had always answered the phone when she rang, even when he'd worked all night at the station, and he'd taken her to a handful of doctor's appointments when she felt too sick to manage alone. He opened doors and pulled out chairs for her. He always paid the bill when they went out. His demeanor was gentle, but there was a seriousness to him, a focus toward his business that she admired. She was growing used to his smooth, russet-colored skin, his rigid long nose, and those dark charcoal eyes. Sure, he had an accent that wasn't entirely attractive. Yes, sometimes his shirts had the lingering smell of a pungent curry dinner he made himself the night before. And OK, he was a little too eager that time a kiss and an accidental brush of the hand meant she had to go home with a sticky patch of wetness on her skirt.

All of this aside, she knew he wasn't just messing around with her the way every other man in her past had.

"Go look at my little Mimi," she encouraged him.

He smiled. "Why the name Mimi? It's different. I like it."

"I chose the name long before I knew there would be a daughter, when I was a child myself. One of my first memories is of watching a black and white rebroadcasting of The Tonight Show, where Mimi Hines sang, 'Till There Was You. It's silly, I know. But I always wanted to name a child Mimi."

"It's not silly at all."

Nazar walked carefully to the bassinet and leaned inside, stretching his neck out of fear that being too close might wake the slumbering babe. "She is so tiny," he said, looking back at Carolyn.

Nazar had only ever seen his younger brother Lut as a baby and he had certainly never been anywhere near a woman who had just given birth. She knew he remembered Lut's delivery only as an event that was wildly difficult on the entire household. It had been chaotic, nothing even remotely as serene as the hospital room he was now standing in.

"They're going to let me take her home this afternoon. Will you be able to give us a lift?" she asked, already knowing the answer.

He moved back over toward her bed and stood awkwardly at the edge.

"At your command," he replied, with a sheepish smile.

Chapter 6

It had been nine weeks since Carolyn and Mimi returned to their shabby little studio apartment following the birth. The flat was free under the Section 8 Housing scheme she had qualified for when she fell pregnant, and the weekly stipend of food stamps kept the two of them from starving. Carolyn couldn't afford much else on the scant monthly welfare allowance she received, but she was grateful to have what she did and even more so when she snuggled up next to Mimi on their futon at night.

Mimi always accompanied Carolyn and Nazar on their Friday night dates. There wasn't any money for a sitter, and even if there had been, Carolyn wasn't ready to be parted from her sweet girl. It wasn't an issue for either since Nazar seemed to be keen on seeing Mimi, and Mimi spent a good sixteen hours a day in peaceful slumber.

"Here, let me carry that," Nazar said, reaching for the sleeping Mimi's carrier as they walked up the steps to Carolyn's second-floor apartment.

She gently passed the carrier to Nazar, relieved to be free of its weight for a few moments.

As they approached, she took the keys from her purse and, after careful examination, she found the right one and slid it into the lock. As she opened the door, Nazar leaned in to kiss her on the cheek and handed the carrier back to Carolyn.

"Would you like to come inside?" Carolyn asked.

Nazar had never been inside her apartment. Before Mimi's birth they had fooled around in his car a bit, but he had been hesitant to even kiss her on the mouth after she had delivered.

"Umm, yeah, if…" he paused nervously. "If you're OK with that. I mean…"

"It's fine, silly," she reassured him, "just don't complain about the mess!"

She flicked on the light switch, and Nazar got his first glimpse of her studio, scarcely the size of his parking space outside. The kitchen to the left was a jumble of avocado Formica and stacks of dirty dishes, the remnants of whatever had been eaten off of them encrusted by at least three days of lingering. Straight through was the living space, possessing nothing more than a sprawled queen-sized futon, a second-hand television with aluminum foil on the antennae, and an explosion of clothes littering the gray carpet.

Carolyn saw the place through his eyes, closed the door behind them, and set the carrier with the sleeping Mimi upon the only clear space on the peeling countertop. She then took Nazar's hand and led him toward the futon.

"Are you sure you…" he started to ask, before Carolyn reached her fingers behind his neck and pulled his lips to hers.

What started as a slow and gentle kiss quickly escalated to a frenzy of squeezing and tugging at each other's clothing. They collapsed together onto the lumpy futon mattress, Carolyn sliding off her cream bra and lace panties while Nazar hastily unfastened the belt to remove his pants. His body felt lean and soft under her fingertips, and she arched her hips to receive him once he had gotten is trousers around his ankles. One, two, three pushes. He expelled himself inside of her with a loud groan, and it was over as quickly as it had begun.

Carolyn rolled onto her side and propped her head up onto her hand, reaching over to smooth a disobedient lock of Nazar's hair from his forehead. He looked over at her and smiled.

"Sorry," he said lazily. "It's supposed to get better with time, right?"

Carolyn burst into with laughter. "I hope so!"

She watched as Nazar turned towards her and allowed his eyes to take in her naked body. The alabaster glow of her skin, her small pink nipples flaking around the edges from Mimi's suckling, the gentle curve of her hips intersecting with a slight patch of light brown, almost blond hair concealing her lady bits. He ran his finger over her slender waist, and she saw him checking out the contrast of his darker skin tone against her milky flesh.

"Do all white women keep this?" he asked, tickling the patch of hair between her thighs.

"What?" she laughed out in surprise, "You mean pubic hair?"

"Yeah. Is that normal? To keep it?"

"Of course it's normal," she retorted. Then she looked down below Nazar's flat stomach and saw that he was as smooth as the day he was born.

"We shave," he said quickly as her eyes started to widen. "It's religious. We have to."

"Oh, so religious now are we?" Carolyn joked, "And what we just did, you have to shave, but you can lie here naked with me?"

Nazar let out a loud guffaw and ignored the last part of her question. "Under here too," he lifted his arm to reveal a smooth, clean armpit.

Laughing, she raised her eyes to meet his and lifted her own arm, "Well, that's not special!"

He pulled her into his arms and kissed her gently on the forehead. "I have to get you and Mimi out of this horrible apartment," he whispered into her cheek. "Come stay with me."

She pulled back and met his eyes again. "It's not horrible," she said defensively. "It's free, it's mine, and it's home. It might not be as glamorous as other apartments, but I have never felt at home anywhere but here."

Nazar sighed and put his hands behind his head. Carolyn had told him before that she had spent the better part of the last few years couch surfing at the homes of her friends and in a host of shelters throughout the Bay Area. No matter how hard she tried to rationalize that a life without a permanent roof over her head was better than staying with either of her feral, nomadic parents, she knew that he couldn't wrap his mind around what it would mean to be so alone. His own parents, his family back home, had been such a fixture in his day to day life. The first time he had ever been parted from anyone in his family was when he left on the flight that brought him to America. Even then, he spoke with his parents two, sometimes three nights a week on the telephone.

"What would your parents think of me living with you?" Carolyn asked tentatively, breaking his concentration.

"It would destroy them," Nazar answered.

So much for that, she thought.

"But we are here and they are there. Don't worry about them. Just think of Mimi...is this the best place to raise her?"

As if in answer to his question, Mimi let out a muffled cry from her position on the counter. Carolyn stood up, grabbing an oversized t-shirt from the floor, and moved to her daughter. She looked into the carrier, just as Mimi reached up to wrap a bolt of Carolyn's hair around her tiny hand. In her heart, she knew this was no place to build a life for her daughter. She didn't know what a shared residence with a man like Nazar would mean for her, but she knew what a nicer home in a better zip code without financial worries could mean for her daughter. Undoing the safety belts securing Mimi in place, she lifted her baby into her arms and turned to Nazar on the futon.

"All right," she said. "We'll move in with you."

The next morning Carolyn stuffed a single suitcase full of the only worldly possessions worth taking, and the three of them left for Nazar's condominium in the affluent Bay Area suburb of San Ramon. The complex had been built onto a hill. As as she walked in, the first thing Carolyn noticed was the floor-to-ceiling windows through the living room that overlooked the canyon.

"This is spectacular," she said, hardly able to believe she would be living there.

"This was the model home they toured buyers through when they were building," Nazar said as if confessing. "So it came furnished."

"It's like from a magazine," Carolyn replied as she ran her fingers across the back of a pristine white leather sofa. She took in the rest of the common living space. It was a sea of white. A high pile, plush carpet ran wall to wall, creating the foundation for a bleached and lacquered armoire, matching coffee and side tables, and a pair of Danish falcon chairs. Sunken down two steps to the right of the living room was a formal dining room with a large, round glass top table and six white fiberglass shell chairs. A streamlined Formica fitted kitchen of champagne gold sat neatly to the side.

"Where is Mimi's room?" Carolyn asked.

"The master bedroom is down the corridor, last door on the right. You can pick from the other two rooms the one you want for Mimi," Nazar replied, pointing down a narrow passage. "The third room you can use for whatever you want. I don't know if you want a sewing room or something."

Carolyn couldn't help but chuckle at this. She had hardly done a domestic task in her life, aside from vacuuming, and only because Mimi seemed to like the firmness of the floor.

"I'll find a use for it," she said.

Nazar brought her suitcase back to the master bedroom and set it down on the floor. Carolyn followed and was rewarded with a second sweeping view of the canyon. She continued walking through a closeted corridor within the suite and into a bathroom that was bigger than her whole Hayward apartment. She sat on the edge of the circular Jacuzzi tub and squinted at her boyfriend. "How on earth can you afford this?" she asked.

"I can't, actually," Nazar replied. "My parents gave me the money to buy it when they realized I would be settling in the states permanently. They also bought the gas station. But really, it is theirs too, so they didn't exactly buy it just for me."

Carolyn raised an eyebrow. "How so?"

"Parents invest all the money they have into their children. The children hopefully are successful, and eventually earn enough to take care of their parents in their old age."

"Couldn't they just invest the money and take care of themselves in their old age?"

"They could, yes. But would you want Mimi to start with nothing as you did, or would you rather give her what you built yourself so she doesn't have to struggle? And in your retirement, you don't struggle either?"

"I can't argue with that logic." Carolyn laughed, put her arms around Nazar's neck, and lifted her head up to kiss him. "Thank you for this," she whispered against his lips.

He kissed her gently and slipped out of her embrace. "There is cash in the drawer by the bed," he said, pointing to a shiny white nightstand with a round, clear acrylic lamp on top. "Go to the grocery store at the bottom of the hill and get what you need. I'll be working until late in the night, but if you need me, you know the number for the station."

He moved down the hallway and picked up his car keys from the slick kitchen countertop. Unbolting the front door, he turned before closing it and said, "I almost forgot, don't answer the phone if it rings. And when you buy groceries - no pork and no alcohol."

The door shut swiftly behind him before Carolyn could find her tongue.

Finally, she shouted at the closed door, "What do you mean - no pork?!"

Chapter
7

On the first Sunday Nazar had taken off in the three weeks since Carolyn and Mimi had moved in, the group crowded into Nazar's flashy red Dodge Challenger and headed to Sunnyvale to buy a stroller and some much needed baby furniture for Mimi's room. She had spent most evenings sharing a bed with them, but after a long night of soothing her after Nazar had rolled over onto her delicate arm in his sleep, they both decided it was time to get her a proper crib.

Pulling up into the parking lot of the giant Toys R Us, Carolyn took the baby carrier that the growing child was almost too big for and lifted it from the vehicle. Together they walked toward the entrance, and Carolyn quickly crossed herself, touching her forehead, then belly, and finally moving her fingers from the right shoulder to the left.

"What the heck are you doing?" Nazar asked.

Carolyn shrugged. It had been more than a decade since she had set foot in a Catholic church, but occasionally the old habits came back at opportune times. "The store is haunted," she said.

"What do you mean the store is haunted?" Nazar asked, stopping in his tracks and turning to her with an unconvinced half smile spreading across his face.

"The store is built over an old apple ranch from the 1800s," she told him. "This was the John Murphey Ranch. A migrant worker named Johnny Johnson moved from Pennsylvania to work on the orchard – Crazy Johnny, they called him. He died chopping wood by a well when the axe slipped and cut into his leg."

Nazar couldn't help but laugh at the serious tone Carolyn had taken. "Go on," he said, clearly amused.

"Crazy Johnny fell in love with Elizabeth, 'Beth' they called her, the ranch owner's daughter. Before Crazy Johnny died, Beth married another man and left the ranch. Now he haunts the aisles, turns on the water taps in the ladies bathroom, and sometimes strokes women's long hair as they shop." Carolyn reached her hand to touch her own hair, and tucked it carefully down the collar of her poplin shirt.

"And you believe this story?" Nazar asked, suppressing his grin.

"I don't know. But I don't want to find out if it's true while I'm in the store."

Nazar let out an exaggerated sigh. "All right. But don't cross yourself. To protect yourself from harm, you say '*A'oodhu bi kalimaat Allah hil-taammah min sharri ma khalaqa*'."

"A whoody what?" Carolyn asked.

"It's Arabic. It means 'I seek refuge in the perfect words of Allah from the evil of that which He has created'."

"Since when do you speak Arabic?"

"I don't. But all prayers – *duas* – are in Arabic. And the Quran is in Arabic, which we never change. So everything we pray and everything we recite is in Arabic."

Carolyn tried to process what he was saying.

"Repeat after me," Nazar continued, stretching out the words phonetically so she could easily repeat them. "*Ah ood-hu bee kalley-mawt..*"

"*Ah ood-hu bee kalley-mawt..*"

"*:Allah hill tah-mah-min...*"

"*:Allah hill tah-mah-min...*"

"*Shah-ree mah khal-a-qa.*"

"*Shah-ree mah khal-a-qa,*" Carolyn smiled. "Now I am double protected."

They entered the store in silence but were quickly consumed by the immediate needs of little Mimi and her bedroom. Soon forgetting Crazy Johnny, they loaded a cart with a top of the line Mutsy stroller, complete with interchangeable bassinet and seat. Also added was a white Jenny Lind model crib and matching changing table that conformed to changes after the new dangers of lead paint were revealed, a pop-up playpen, and a host of accessories and playthings to keep Mimi occupied as she started to grow.

Carolyn was once again struck by Nazar's generosity as he paid for the heap of baby goods and loaded them into the trunk of his car. They drove out of the parking lot, the back of the Challenger so weighed down it scraped over a speed bump on the way out.

Laughing, Carolyn pushed an ejected cassette tape back into the car's built-in deck, humming along with Bee-Gee's tunes throughout the long ride home.

The Color Book of Indian Cooking had become Carolyn's kitchen bible. After weeks of enduring omelets, baked potatoes, soggy spaghetti, and an assortment of canned dinners, Nazar bought the cookbook in the hope that she might be able to put something palatable together.

"My mother would proudly argue that food prepared for Pakistani meals was definitely not Indian, but it's close enough and better than another night of burnt toast and sweet corn," Nazar teased.

Carolyn gave him a playful pinch on the arm. Together, they unpacked a bag of dried herbs and spices and put them on the rack inside a kitchen cupboard.

"Let's make the first meal together," he said, putting two ripe tomatoes into the refrigerator. "A joint effort."

"Why? So you can tell me how your Ammi used to do it this way – or that way?" Carolyn joked. She liked how the word Ammi rolled off her tongue, but couldn't imagine calling a mother anything but Mom. She certainly wouldn't want to be called anything but Mom herself.

"Actually, Ammi rarely cooked." Nazar said.

"If your mom never cooked, then who made all these meals you talk about missing from home?" Carolyn turned toward him. "Did you have little Punjabi kitchen elves?"

Nazar let out a loud laugh, holding onto the side of the counter and almost knocking down a jar of ginger paste. "Punjabi kitchen elves?" he snorted. "We had a cook."

Carolyn raised her eyebrows at this. "A cook?" she asked, surprised. "A cook? You had a cook?"

"We had a servant who started as a maid, but she also cooked. When another maid was hired, the first became mostly a full time cook. It's really normal there."

"They weren't…" Carolyn asked slowly, afraid of what the answer might be, "they weren't like slaves, were they?"

"No, no," Nazar answered, "not at all. They were paid, and they lived in their own part of the house. One even had a son who grew up with us. He's now the guard at our gate, I think. Still should be."

Carolyn was relieved to hear her boyfriend wasn't a keeper of slaves, but her curiosity about his upbringing and the idea of actually having servants both perplexed and intrigued her. "Maids, a cook….and a gatekeeper?"

"It's not as glamorous as it all sounds. It's totally normal there."

"It still sounds glamorous, Nazar. I can't imagine growing up with servants. What was it like?" Carolyn asked, curious about this world so far removed from her own upbringing. The only time anyone cooked for her or washed her dishes was on the rare occasions she ate at a restaurant. It was impossible to imagine a team of servants walking the halls of their apartment, cooking, cleaning, and doing whatever else a servant did.

"It was easier, not having to worry about anything," Nazar answered. "I mean, of course we still had things to worry about, but I never had to wash or cook anything until the day I moved to America. You can imagine how lost I was. I was actually quite upset at myself for never paying attention when I first came."

Carolyn looked down to the jar of garam masala in her hands. She had lived in America her whole life and was only today really trying to cook for the first time. "I never had anyone to do anything for me, and you still picked it up faster than I did." She sighed, setting down the spice jar.

Nazar walked over to her and wrapped his arms around her waist. He kissed her on the forehead. "Are you sure you don't want me to help you with the meal?"

Carolyn shook her head. "I want to do it myself," she said. She knew if she was going to learn that she would have to just dive head first into it. "But I hope you aren't expecting it to be as good as your cooks'."

"I expect it to be better!" Nazar replied, reaching out toward the cookbook.

Carolyn picked up the book and swatted his arm. "Get out of my kitchen, you old brute!"

Nazar held up his hands in surrender and walked out of the kitchen. Carolyn turned back to her cookbook.

Pakistani food, which Nazar said was almost indistinguishable from Indian food, was only something she had eaten as a child. Her mother, who was around at that time, had gone through a stage where all things exotic were essential to her lifestyle, and Carolyn had had her palate tempted by a wide range of cuisines. Her favorite had been *dim sum* at the Hang Ah Tea Room in San Francisco's Chinatown. Plump, steamed mouthfuls of dumplings were stuffed with things she didn't want to know. She also had fond memories at House of India in Ghirardelli Square, which had been recently rebranded to Gaylord India. One of the foods she hoped to recreate from her childhood excursions was a spicy *chole masala* over fragrant basmati rice. Her mother's itinerant existence might not have made for good parenting, but it did open Carolyn up to flavors and experiences her friends at the time knew nothing about.

Carolyn opened the book. She carefully flipped through the glossy pages looking for the *chole masala* recipe, a fiery chickpea curry. Just a few pages in, the dish leapt out from left side of the book in a full page photo. She ran her fingers over the ingredients and went to take what she needed from the spices she had just put away. As she selected the cumin, chili, coriander seeds, cardamom, and dried bay leaves, the phone on the wall in the kitchen let out a loud ring.

She knew the phone was off limits unless it was their coded ring. Two rings, disconnect, one ring again. This was the string of whirring rings that were familiar to her twice a week. It meant Nazar's parents were calling from Pakistan.

"*Assalamualeikum*," Nazar answered from a phone in their bedroom. All the phone cords in the house extended across the length of the rooms they were placed in, and she heard the door close softly so the call wouldn't be interrupted by a crying Mimi if she happened to wake up. The rule was that when his parents called, it had to be silent. There could be nothing to expose to his family the fact that Nazar wasn't living alone.

As they often did, the calls became slightly heated, and Carolyn could hear a muffled change of tone carry down the corridor. Nazar never raised his voice to his parents when he spoke to them, but he had a tendency to talk faster and become agitated, the way a child does when they have done something wrong and are trying to talk their way out of it. He frequently ended the calls looking flustered and becoming melancholy in the immediate aftermath. She never asked what the problem was but had more than once wished she spoke Urdu so she could, at the very least, eavesdrop.

She carried on measuring out her spices and opened a can of chickpeas. Nazar had raised an eyebrow at her when she selected a can off the shelf over the bags of uncooked chickpeas, but she had decided to take shortcuts, at least in the beginning, whenever they presented themselves.

"Why soak chickpeas for three hours in baking soda when you can just open a can and pop them in a saucepan?" she had asked at the store. She had easily convinced him that it was still cooking, just without wasting time on steps that could be avoided.

As she was chopping a tomato and adding it as the final ingredient to her aromatic pot, Nazar reentered the room.

"Everything all right?" she asked.

Nazar shrugged and let out a sigh, making his way over to the white leather sofa. "It's fine," he replied, unconvincingly.

Carolyn put the lid on her bubbling *chole masala* and reduced the heat dial to low to allow the chickpeas to simmer. Walking over to the couch, she put her hand on his knee as she sat down next to him.

He looked over and gave her a half smile. Not wanting to push him into discussing something he wasn't ready for, she leaned forward and buried her head into his chest. He kissed the top of her hair, and they sat in silence, allowing the scent of Carolyn's first attempt at Pakistani cooking to waft pleasurably throughout the apartment.

Chapter
8

Mimi sat on the white carpet collecting rings of Cheerios she had dumped from her cup onto the thick berber and popping them into her mouth.

"Mimi!" Carolyn snapped. "No, no little peanut! No, no on the carpet!"

She knelt down to pick up the remaining hoops of wheat and poured them back into the green plastic cup. The two-year-old looked up at her with big blue eyes and reached her chubby hand forward.

"Mimi's!" She said excitedly, a bit of Cheerio projecting from her mouth and onto the floor.

Carolyn couldn't help but laugh. The strawberry blond ringlets of her daughter's hair bounced as she nodded her little head in a yes motion. She'd have to vacuum the rug before Nazar got home, but she knew it would be late, and she'd have plenty of time. She walked with the cup back over to the kitchen counter and began to open the small pile of envelopes she had collected from the letterbox. A bill, a solicitation from the local ice cream shop with a free kid cone for Mimi's birthday, and...

"What the...?" Carolyn asked herself quietly, as a glossy photo floated from the torn envelope to the white linoleum. She turned the envelope over. It was from Pakistan, and she hadn't realized she had opened a letter from Nazar's family.

She bent down to pick up the photo and turned it around to reveal a sepia toned image of a stunning girl no older than twenty in an ornate, traditional beaded Pakistani dress. Her glossy black hair was tied into a fishtailed braid that rested over her slender shoulders. She was adorned in a heavy gold necklace and matching chandelier earrings, complementing the fleck of gold on her delicate Roman, slant tipped nose. Her eyes pierced

Carolyn with their cool amber, highlighted by the tone of the photo.

She reached for the envelope and emptied it of its contents. Two more photos of two more young girls around the same age were exposed. One was full color - an attractive girl sitting on the floor, her slim knees to her chest and draped in delicate lemon yellow chiffon. Her feminine, slight hands were arranged across her covered knees to display a procession of glass yellow and silver bangles up her arms. The color of the photo was set off in a backdrop of strung carnelians matching her bracelets and gown, hung across a wall behind her. Unlike the girl in the first photo, this one had a long, dark golden-brown plait that hung down her back and coiled onto the flowers around her.

The final photo was a headshot, also in full color. Large, almond-shaped eyes with a heavy spray of lashes stared out at Carolyn. This girl's skin was milky and much fairer than the other two, with a sharp, exotic nose and thick, full lips painted with a soft gloss. A willowy hand rested under her chin, her knuckle barely grazing the soft curve of her chin.

Carolyn set the photos down and picked up the letter enclosed in the same envelope. The neat, beautifully scrolled handwriting of Nazar's mother revealed nothing of the letters contents. It was a language she couldn't speak and an alphabet completely different from the script of any English words. An elegant cursive of loops and squiggly, indistinguishable lines.

She couldn't wait until Nazar got home to talk to him. She didn't know what these photos were for, but she knew his mother was deeply religious and wouldn't have sent pictures of beautiful young women for his visual entertainment. They couldn't be family members, as Nazar had told her before that segregation of the genders was commonplace and the photos contained singular girls completely devoid of any other family members. They could only be for one purpose.

Carolyn picked up the handset from the kitchen wall and spun the rotary dials with the numbers to the gas station.

"Gas and Go, how can I help?" Nazar answered.

"Nazar, it's Carolyn. Are you busy?"

"Not really. Sam just came in, so I was going to stock the cigarettes. Everything OK?"

"I don't know," Carolyn said, realizing how nervous she sounded. "A letter came from your mom. I accidentally opened it and it has pictures of women in it. Young women, Nazar."

Silence. Nazar cleared his throat and let out a sigh.

"What's going on, Nazar? Who are these girls?"

"Just....everything is fine, Carolyn. I'll come home to talk to you."

"Now?"

"Yes. I'm leaving now."

A lump in Carolyn's throat began to form, and she felt sick. Nazar not having an easy answer and wanting to come home to talk couldn't be a good sign.

The next twenty-five minutes dragged on, and the ticking of the clock rattled in Carolyn's head. She wiped down the kitchen counter with a scouring sponge for the third time, avoiding the pile of painful, face down photos. Mimi had rolled over to her side and fallen asleep on the floor. Her cheek spread against the shag carpet, and Carolyn knew her daughter would wake up with little indents on her face. This made her smile, and for a moment was a welcome distraction. Carolyn had been blissfully happy the last two years living without any worry under Nazar's protection. He doted on Mimi and came home frequently with little treats. Mimi looked to Nazar as a father, and it came as a shock to them both when the first words out of her mouth were da-da.

There was the jingle of a key outside and then the door slowly opened. Nazar entered the apartment and set his keys and empty Tupperware lunchbox on the countertop. His black hair was soaking wet, and droplets of rain clung to his thick lashes and ran down his long nose. Nodding toward Carolyn, he removed his drenched tan, fur lined jacket and set it carefully across the counter. His powder blue mock turtleneck shirt was dry, and Carolyn was thankful that under all that damp he had a layer of comfort.

"Where's Mimi?" Nazar asked.

Carolyn pointed to the mound of pink taffeta and strawberry curls on the floor. "She fell asleep in her favorite spot."

Nazar smiled and met Carolyn's eyes. She glanced down at the stack of envelopes. Nazar's eyes followed. Without lifting the photos to look at them, he pushed them lightly to the side and looked up at Carolyn again.

"I don't know where to start," he said.

"Start by telling me who they are and why your mom is sending you their photographs," Carolyn replied, crossing her arms across her chest. "Are they potential brides or something?"

"Shall we sit down?"

"Oh my God," Carolyn said, her eyes beginning to brim with tears. "Is it that serious that you think we need to sit down?"

Nazar reached his hand out and squeezed her arm. "You don't need to worry, Carolyn. It's just a long story, really complicated. It'll be better if we sit."

His voice was soothing and didn't ring of defensiveness, which put Carolyn at ease. She knew he cared deeply for her and Mimi, and she also trusted him completely. He said she didn't need to worry. She exhaled the breath she hadn't realized she was holding in her clenched chest.

They made their way through the living room, past a sleeping Mimi, and stepped down into the sunken dining room. It had been a clean and lavish setup when Carolyn and Mimi had moved in, but was now littered with Crayola crayons and bits of scribbled paper. Not all the markings had stayed on paper and lines of pink and green and purple marked the glass tabletop. Sinking into one of the shell chairs, Carolyn idly scraped at the crayon wax on the glass with a long manicured scarlet fingernail.

She looked up at Nazar across from her. "Well?" she asked.

Nazar brought his hand around the back of his neck and rubbed gently, reclining into his seat.

"I don't know if you will understand this or how to explain it to you," he started, "but I need you to stay calm and just hear me out."

The calm Carolyn had felt moments before evaporated from her body and she was once again filled with dread.

"You say what you need to say Nazar, but don't tell me how to respond to it or how to feel."

He nodded. "Where I come from, our parents usually take the lead in deciding who we are going to marry. They don't know I am in a relationship with you Carolyn, and so, obviously, at my age - with a home and business of my own and the means to support a wife and family - they think it's time for me to settle down. It sounds strange to you, I know, but it is the way of life where I am from."

Carolyn kept her composure as she felt her stomach lurch. She couldn't speak. She couldn't feel. Her mind was racing. Confusion. Fear.

"The calls from home," he carried on, "I'm sure you have heard the tone even if you didn't understand the words."

Carolyn nodded.

"They want me to come home. To get married."

She couldn't hold it anymore. Bursting into tears, Carolyn asked in a high pitched squeal, "So you are leaving us, then?"

Nazar reached his hand across the table and wound his fingers through hers. "No baby, I love you."

There it was. The three words she had desperately hoped to hear for the last two years that he had never before uttered. She lifted her swollen eyes to meet his. "You do?" she asked, her voice weak and quiet, her heart pounding in her chest.

"I do," he replied.

"I love you too," she said softly.

He squeezed her fingers and released them, relaxing back in his chair. He waited for a moment before proceeding cautiously with his next question.

"Would you ever consider becoming a Muslim?" he asked.

Carolyn shrugged. She didn't know what it meant – to be a Muslim. Nazar never prayed or celebrated anything besides Christmas and Easter with her, decorating the tree together and helping her wrap gifts from Santa and place baskets from the Easter bunny for Mimi against the fireplace. Aside from giving up pork and alcohol, there had been no change in her daily life and those had been easy concessions to make in her mind to share her life with this man that she loved.

"If you became a Muslim, and if we raised Mimi and any kids we might have together as Muslims, we could get married."

Carolyn's heart almost leapt from her chest. Married? Was that possible? This wonderful man who took such great care of her and her daughter – he would marry her and they could become a proper family with an honest future? Her body filled with hope and she felt a smile light up her face. The thought of having Nazar's children, of being his wife, brought more happiness to her than she thought she could bear.

"I have always considered myself spiritual but not really religious," she said. "I was raised Catholic but not in the church, so it never really mattered much to me."

"Islam and Christianity share a lot of the same values and beliefs, and Muslims even believe in the virgin birth of Jesus, peace be upon him, but not as a savior. We believe him to be a Prophet. But let's not get into that now. It's a big decision, and I understand if you need time to think about it."

"Your mom will accept me if I am a Muslim?" Carolyn asked.

"No, not really," he said honestly. "It's bigger than that, Carolyn."

"She doesn't care if you are happy or not?"

"It isn't about being happy. Marriage in Pakistan isn't just about joining two people. It's about creating alliances between two families, or strengthening the bond of your own."

"Your own? Like bonding with your parents by marrying who they want?"

"No, by marrying from the extended family. My older brother Safwat, he married our first cousin Iqra, who was raised with us like a sister. My parents are first cousins, and so were Iqra's parents. There are no other first cousins for me to marry, but those girls in the pictures, two are third or fourth cousins. One isn't related to me, but her family is from the same caste and has the same social standing and financial background as my own."

"Marrying cousins?" Carolyn felt disgusted. "That's like in the olden days of the south. And you didn't answer my question – don't they want you to be happy?"

"I probably would be happy, Carolyn. Not like how I am with you, but in time, I would find happiness with someone of my parents choosing. We all do. My parents are happy. My brother and Iqra are happy. My aunt and uncle were happy. Even if there is no fairy-tale ending, like most people even here, you power through for the kids and for the good of the whole family. In the end you might not have a burning passion, but you do have companionship and children you adore. There are different kinds of love, Carolyn. But happiness is something you build."

"I don't understand how you could be happy getting married to someone you don't know."

"I don't expect you to understand," he said, "but it doesn't change the way it works and has worked throughout the whole of history. Aside from you, nobody knows me better than my parents. You and I moved in together just like a married couple without knowing each other hardly at all, and it has worked. How is that different from my parents choosing a girl for me based on my personality and who they think I would make a good match with, and me marrying them and moving in just as quickly?"

It was a valid point that Carolyn had a hard time arguing, even if it sounded strange to her. Still, she had the option of leaving if she and Nazar hadn't gotten along. Divorce was a lot more serious than just packing up her few possessions and moving out.

"If your parents decide who you marry, then why is your mom sending you photographs?"

"They don't make the decision entirely on their own. In poorer areas, it works like that, but not in our family or in our circle. A mother makes inquiries to other mothers about their daughters, if she knows or hears good things about them and their family. Once she narrows it down to a few, she shows her son who is she thinks is best. For example, my mom sent me these photographs. I would maybe choose one that I like the look of, then go back to Pakistan and meet with my parents, the girl, and her parents for a casual tea. I might be able to talk to her – although not date like here. It's all chaperoned. If I like her, our families might meet again one or two, sometimes more, times. Then, with my urging, our parents would discuss the match seriously. And we would probably get married within a few months, or weeks."

Carolyn's head was spinning. It didn't sound as bad as she imagined, just showing up at the altar – do they have altars? – to meet the person you had to spend the rest of your life with. It didn't matter. It wasn't her life, and Nazar wasn't going to do it that way. He had chosen her. He had chosen Mimi. She just needed to figure out what happened next.

"So why would it matter if I became a Muslim?" she asked. "And what would happen if I said yes, and we got married?"

"It would still be impossible for her to understand, but if we were married, she would have to at least accept it. She wouldn't accept it at all if I married a non-Muslim."

"You keep saying she…what about your dad in all this?"

"My dad is quiet, and my mom sort of runs the show."

Carolyn laughed. "So some things then are universal!"

"Yes." Nazar joined in the laughter. "I suppose they are."

He stood up and moved to the chair beside her, taking both her hands in his. "So," he asked, "will you marry me?"

"Yes," Carolyn answered, smiling. It was the easiest answer to the clearest question she had ever given anyone in her whole life.

Chapter
9

The wedding ceremony was like nothing
Carolyn had ever witnessed before. Instead of being
swathed in the flowing, puffy white satin she had
dreamed of since childhood, she was shrouded in a black
abaya and headscarf that concealed every strand of her
golden hair. An Imam – the Islamic version of a pastor –
had entered the home with two bearded men Carolyn
hadn't met before. They came attired in *kaftan*-style long
shirts over loose pants that tapered at the ankles, and
caps over the tops of their cropped hair that looked to
Carolyn like a Jewish yarmulke, except instead of sitting

on the crown of their heads, they neatly stretched across their foreheads and back over the crown. All three kept their eyes lowered as they stepped into the apartment, removed their shoes, and moved past her without acknowledgment into the living room with Nazar. Following behind was a robust, matronly woman of about fifty-five dressed in a colorful, bright mauve and floral version on Carolyn's own outfit. She stayed back awkwardly in the kitchen, running her finger between her chin and the cloth that felt like it was choking her.

"Ya Allah!" the woman shouted at Caroyln happily, patting her cheek. "So drab in black for your wedding day! Who pick this?" she asked, lifting the bottom of Carolyn's headscarf and rubbing the scratchy wool between her worn fingers.

Carolyn nodded her head toward the culprit of the fashion debacle. Nazar had briefed her on what would transpire and had helped her dress into the black coverings, insisting the somber outfit was exactly what she needed to be in.

"Tuk, tuk," the woman said, clicking her tongue. "You look nice even in this, with your fair skin and light eyes, *mashaAllah*."

Carolyn blushed. She certainly didn't feel like she looked nice, but the prideful stare Nazar had passed over her when he had finished securing her scarf didn't escape her notice. It was like he was seeing her for the first time, and his gaze lingered much longer than it ever had before. "Beautiful, *mashaAllah*," he had whispered, almost breathless.

"My name Varisha," the woman said, jabbing her finger into her own chest. "My husband Tanveer," she pointed to the Imam seated on the couch next to Nazar, "and you know my son Samit." She winked.

Carolyn didn't have to rack her brain to try and remember who the son she was supposed to know was. The truth was neither she nor Nazar had any real friends, so she definitely didn't know Samit, and was surprised even that Nazar was able to round up this small bridal party.

Sensing Carolyn's confusion, Varisha clarified, "Samit is Sam. Sam work for Nazar."

"Ah yes, Sam!" Carolyn nodded in recognition. She rarely went to the gas station and didn't drive, so while she knew of Sam she couldn't say she actually knew him. They had never met.

"Your family is here?" Varisha looked around, half expecting Carolyn's Texan father to emerge from a closet somewhere.

"They aren't." Carolyn said. She had considered inviting her parents but later decided against it. She didn't know where her mother was or how to reach her, and didn't know how to explain the relationship or a roomful of bearded men to her father, who probably would've arrived with a date dressed for a nightclub. The wedding was also arranged in the span of ten days, not difficult, given its simplicity and it being held – without food or any reception – in their living room.

Varisha raised her eyebrows. "Tuk, tuk," she clucked again with her tongue.

"My daughter is here though, sleeping in the bedroom." Carolyn pointed down the corridor and then raised her finger to her mouth in a mock quiet motion.

"Your daughter?" Varisha asked, her eyes widening. "You have….."

"Carolyn, come on over," Nazir motioned for her to join the men in the living room.

"Tuk, tuk," Varisha clucked again to herself.

Keeping her eyes on the floor in front of her, Carolyn made her way to the living room. She was excited to be united with Nazar as his wife but the foreign customs and bewildering ceremony was almost terrifying. She took a deep breath and stood next to her fiancé.

The Imam, Tanveer, peered at her from the corner of his eye. "Are you ready to say *shahada*?"

Nazar had explained before the wedding – or *Nikkah*, as he called it – that she would make her testimony and become a Muslim. It would be in Arabic, and he promised it would be said slowly so she could repeat it properly. She felt her tongue swell in her mouth.

"I am," she said in almost a whisper.

Tanveer cleared his throat. "I will say it once so you hear it on your ear, then say it slowly in parts for you to repeat, yes?"

Carolyn nodded *yes*.

"*La'ilaha illa-llah, Muhammadun rasulu-llah*," Tanveer recited the Kalima in a clear, loud, confident voice.

There is no god but Allah, and Muhammad is the messenger of Allah.

It sounded lyrical to Carolyn's ear. Beautiful. Calming.

"*La ilaha*," Tanveer said slowly.

"*La ilaha*," Carolyn repeated.

"*illa-llah*"

"*illa-llah*"

"*Muhammadun*"

"*Muhammadun*"

"*rasulu-llah*."

"*rasulu-llah*," Carolyn repeated the last of the Kalima.

"*SubhanAllah*," Tanveer said, putting his hand on Nazar's shoulder. *Glory be to Allah.*

Carolyn smiled to herself. She was a Muslim, and now she was about to become Nazar's wife.

Tanveer picked up a large document written in the scrolled text Carolyn recognized from Nazar's letters from home, although this was clearly written by a different hand. Under each line was an English translation. "Nikkah-nama" was printed boldly across the top. He turned to a man on the other side of the room and said something in Urdu, Nazar's language, that Carolyn didn't understand.

"Since you are without a male Muslim family member to stand for you, my brother Darim has come as your *Wali* and as a witness," Tanveer said, motioning toward the man who came forward. He was short and darker skinned than anyone else in the room, his graying beard resting against a thick silver chain around his soft neck.

"*Assalamualeikum*," he said briskly to Carolyn.

"*Waleikum-salam*," Carolyn replied, exactly as Nazar had taught her.

Tanveer proceeded to ask a series of questions in rapid succession that Carolyn knew nothing about, prompting her guardian for the occasion to grunt in acceptance to each inquiry. Something about a *Mahr* – money it sounded like to Carolyn – and general acceptance of the terms of the contract. Calling a marriage a contract seemed cold and businesslike to Carolyn, but nothing about this wedding was familiar to her. Because she wasn't a virgin, she was required to verbally accept Nazar as her husband, which she did with some degree of embarrassment. In a room full of religious men having to acknowledge that she accepted the marriage terms on the grounds of being a previously unmarried mother wasn't done without some humiliation.

Her guardian and Nazar signed the document and the pen was handed to her. She made her mark next to the signature of the *wali*. Tanveer gave Nazar a heavy handed pat on the back and the men all broke into laughter and swift chatter in Urdu. From behind her, Carolyn felt the tug of her sleeve and turned to see a beaming Varisha, who had been all but forgotten about until that moment. Varisha leaned forward and kissed Carolyn on each cheek.

Carolyn bowed to look at Nazar, her husband, who caught her gaze and winked at her. Her heart filled with pride and hope for a bright future for her and their little family of three.

Chapter
10

Ring, ring.

Ring, ring.

Carolyn waited to hear the unfamiliar voice of her father on the other end of the line.

"Hello," he answered with a southern twang, his voice gruff from years of inhaling cigarettes and hard living.

"Dad?" Carolyn said.

"Is that my favorite daughter?" he asked, his abrasive tone softening as a heavy cough rang through the handset into Carolyn's ear.

Carolyn laughed. "How are ya, Pop?"

"I'm doing really good, Carol. How's the baby?"

"Not exactly a baby anymore, but Mimi is doing very well."

"I meant to call you for Christmas, but it all just got away from me."

It always got away from him, Carolyn thought. A year could pass as quickly as a week in the time it took for her dad to pick up a phone to call. It had been that way since her mother discovered his infidelities when Carolyn was about Mimi's age – not that her mother had much cause to complain. She had her own string of affairs, and had it not been for Carolyn's strong resemblance to the man she called father, his paternity could have been called into question years ago.

"You always mean to call, Pop, but you never do."

"Hey, hey, hey," her dad replied, "you can dial a phone number just as easily as your old man."

Carolyn sighed. She hadn't called for an argument. "All right, Pop," she conceded. "All right."

"How is my grandbaby?" he asked.

"She's so big now, Pop, and growing so fast. She's saying words and toddling around the house. Just last night she climbed out of her crib and came into bed with Nazar and me."

As soon as the words came out of her mouth she remembered that reason for the call and instantly regretted her slip of tongue.

"Nay-who?" he asked, pronouncing the first part of his name with a Texan drawl.

"Nazar, Pop. I got married."

Her father was momentarily quiet on the other end. "You got yourself married?" he asked, his surprise unmasked.

"I did," she said with confidence.. "He's a good man, Pop."

"What kind of name is Nay-zar?"

"It's pronounced Nah-zar. He's from Pakistan. It's like India," she lied, "kind of."

"What the…" he trailed off at a loss for words.

"It doesn't matter, Pop. He's amazing with Mimi and me – really looks after us. He owns a nice apartment and has his own business. You'd like him."

"Is he from that religion that makes women dress in those big blue things? The one that covers all their eyes and such? Are you married to one of them men who takes innocent, hard-working Americans hostage?"

"That's Iran, Pop, not Pakistan." She knew her father watched the same news everyone else in the country watched. The American embassy in Tehran was under siege, and fifty-two diplomats were currently being held hostage by Muslim students supporting their revolution. It was something she and Nazar had discussed at great length, and Nazar had shown complete support for the hostages and not the slightest degree of sympathy to the perpetrators. She saw nothing of her husband in the men with automatic rifles, their faces and heads covered in checkered scarves, demanding retribution from the west for their unwanted influence.

"It's all the same to me!" he shouted. "If that Ay-rab thinks he can just come over here and get into bed with my child…"

"He's not an Arab!" She interrupted defensively. "And even if he were, he's not what you think they are! He's gentle and kind – he loves us!"

"It's all tomato-tamahto to me, girl! These men are dangerous! You can't just marry any old…"

Carolyn could feel her blood boiling and slammed down the phone, cutting the call off abruptly. She wasn't going to listen to her father's ignorant rant about a man he knew nothing about. Who was he anyway to all of the sudden show any misguided concern for her? She hadn't heard from the man since Mimi had been born – and hadn't taken any interest in her life or his granddaughter's life for the past two years.

She was seething in anger and grateful Mimi and Nazar had gone out on the balcony to allow her privacy for the call. Carolyn had been so anxious about Nazar telling his parents about the marriage, which he still had yet to do. It never occurred to her that her own parents might have a similarly appalling reaction. Her father was almost 1500 miles away in Dallas, but he might have well been on the moon for all the time he spent with her.

Ring, ring the phone sent off, pulling her from her thoughts.

"Hello?" she answered, her annoyance still rattling her voice.

There was a static silence on the other line, followed by the hollowed out voice of a woman on the other end.

"*Assalamualeikum*," the woman said, so softly Carolyn had to strain to hear her. It only took a split second for Carolyn to realize she had answered a call she wasn't supposed to, having presumed her father was calling her back. She knew he wouldn't – too proud to ever acknowledge he was wrong – and swore silently to herself for answering.

"One moment, please," she said slowly. Setting the handset down on the counter, she went to the balcony to her husband.

"Nazar, I'm so sorry," she said quietly, her hands shaking. "I think your mother is on the phone."

He and Mimi looked to her in unison with wildly different expressions. Nazar's usually calm face transformed into a look of quiet horror, his eyes widening and his cheeks turning red.

Mimi smiled widely, "Mama I pway wif dis!" she squealed, holding up a red Matchbox Corvette. Nazar had brought it home from the station knowing Mimi preferred anything with wheels over the Barbie dolls Carolyn had tried to play with her.

"Right now?" Nazar asked quietly.

"Yes," she said. "I'm so sorry, Nazar. I just hung up on my father and thought he was calling back."

Nazar let out an exaggerated sigh that ended with a slight whimper. "Here goes," he said.

Carolyn moved past him, keeping her head low to avoid his gaze and bent down next to her little daughter and the car. The sliding door closed behind him as he went through the living room and into the kitchen, and picked up the phone from where its resting place on the counter.

Mimi rolled the car back and forth across the painted white wood slats on the balcony. Carolyn ran a finger across the girl's soft curls and peered in through the glass.

The conversation between Nazar and his mother was indecipherable through the double glazed glass door, not that Carolyn would've understood what was being said anyway. His shoulders slumped, Nazar's lips moved slowly, and she could only assume he was explaining why a woman had answered his phone.

The next fifteen minutes dragged on like an entire afternoon before Carolyn couldn't stomach being outside anymore.

"Do you want to play in your room, Peanut?" she asked Mimi.

Without waiting for a reply, Carolyn slid the door open and let Mimi toddle past her into the apartment. Mimi waved the car around her leisurely and walked toward her bedroom with her toy drifting on make believe clouds in her wake.

Nazar had moved to the couch and his forehead rested between his hands, the phone propped between his cheek and shoulder. She took a seat next to him and watched patiently as her husband replied in malleable tones to the shrieking voice on the other end of the line. He kept his composure in a way Carolyn could never do and could only attribute it to the molding of the woman he was clearly disappointing. He had never spoken a single word of ill against his parents or his brothers, and she couldn't begin to imagine the distress the breaking of this news of his marriage would cause.

After what felt like an eternity, Nazar stood up and put the handset of the phone back into its cradle on the pristine kitchen wall.

"What happened?" she asked.

He looked at her, eyes glazed over – not from crying – but red with strain and worry. "We need to get you and Mimi passports," he said, his words strained. "We're going to Pakistan."

"We're going to…" her words trailed off.

"Pakistan," he said smoothly. "We're going to Pakistan. All of us."

"What? Nazar…how can we possibly go to Pakistan?" She had never been across the California border into Mexico. Pakistan? Of course she assumed his parents might eventually come to visit them in the Bay Area, but in her wildest dreams she never imagined going there.

"It'll be fine," Nazar said in his most comforting tone, "you'll actually really like it."

"Why do we have to go there?" she asked, bewildered. "Why can't they come here? When would we go? For how long?" The questions whirled around in her head and fired out of her mouth faster than she could formulate them.

"We have to go because I've married without their knowledge or consent, and it's the least I can do. It will only be for a couple weeks. They have to meet you and Mimi."

"Why can't they come here?" she asked again, her voice exposing the rising panic in her chest.

125

"I need you to understand something," he said, sitting next to her and taking her hands in his. "It's an enormous blow, me getting married this way. They cannot even begin understand it, and they won't until they have seen you with their own eyes. Even then, they may never understand. But more than that, this looks terrible to the rest of the family and everyone that knows them. If a son marries, it must be at the will of his parents. If we do not go there, my parents will never be able to hold their heads up outside the house again. People will laugh at them for raising a son who ran off and married a foreigner without their knowledge. We have to go. I cannot hurt them in that way too."

Carolyn's head was spinning. "So we just show up and everything is all right?"

Finally, Nazar smiled, and his face relaxed. He looked at her with calm eyes and squeezed her fingertips.

"It's not quite that easy," he said. "We will go and have a *Walima* – like a wedding reception. My parents need to meet you, and they need to have this reception to show the world it wasn't all done in secret. It's *sunnah* to publicize the marriage with a reception. It gives the appearance of acceptance, even if, like in this case, it is only outward."

"So they don't accept it?"

"They don't yet but they will," he assured her, "in time, and when they have met you and gotten to know you. You have to trust me, Carolyn. Do you trust me?"

"I trust you," she whispered. She wrapped her arms around his neck, and he pulled her into an embrace. "You're going to love being looked after and cooked for. You're going to have such a grand adventure, and Mimi will be adored." he breathed into her hair. "I promise."

Chapter
11

The simple act of getting off the airplane was an assault on all of Carolyn's senses. The combination of extreme heat, noise, dust, and vibrant flashes of color on the clothes of the people who rushed toward them as they stepped onto the tarmac, it was overwhelming after twenty-eight hours without sleep. Nazar had attired her back into the black *abaya* she had worn on their wedding day – without the headscarf – and the heat slapped against her like a heavy hand. It became immediately clear that neither she nor Mimi were expected by most of the people in the chattering group. She stepped forward to hand Nazar a woven pink and white hobo bag containing Mimi's travel toys, and several women clucked in confusion when they realized he had come with a woman and child in tow. Nazar reached over to take the sleeping child from her arms. His eyes searched the swarm of approaching family members and lit up when they landed on an older couple emerging from its interior. In an instant they were engulfed into the mass of bodies and Mimi woke up, looking around in uncertainty before letting out a terrified whimper.

Carolyn reached over to stroke the warm cheek of her daughter, and she was at once soothed with the contact and realization she was in Nazar's safe arms. She buried her face into Nazar's neck, and they were both swallowed up by a flurry of colorful silk.

A hand on Carolyn's elbow made her jump for a moment before looking to her right. A stunning woman not much older than she smiled warmly and leaned in toward her in the crush.

"Nazar's wife, no?" she asked pleasantly, her white teeth gleaming against smooth wheatish skin. Her glossy black hair was swept back into a long braid, and a beaded *dupatta* of vibrant orange framed her effervescent complexion and draped down to conceal the small bulge of her pregnant belly. "I am Iqra. I am your sister."

Carolyn impulsively moved in and hugged this woman whose smile warmed her to the core. It was a friendly face in a sea of uncertainty, and it was enough to nearly make her cry in relief. Iqra giggled in Carolyn's embrace and when she was released, her amber eyes were glowing with palpable affection for her new sister-in-law.

From within the crowd, Nazar pulled the women toward him and the couple beside him.

"Ammi and Abbu," he said excitedly, motioning toward a hunched man and an elegantly attired woman.

Carolyn stepped forward with her arms outstretched, and the man took her pale hands into his. His salt and pepper hair was combed back neatly, and his black eyes sparkled at her. His skin was weathered and tired, but lightened significantly when his thin lips spread into a broad smile.

"*Assalamualeikum*," Carolyn said returning the smile.

"Aha!" Abbu said in excitement, "*Waleikumsalam*!"

"*Assalamualeikum*," the soft voice of the graceful woman beside him let out, unsmiling, but not altogether unfriendly.

"*Waleikumsalam*," Carolyn answered back.

Nazar's mother was a vision of elegance in a heavily embroidered russet brown and gold embroidered *salwar kameez*. Her fair skin and composure did nothing to give away any discomfort to the heat despite being in a dress that looked like it belonged on a Hollywood red carpet. Carolyn was immediately self conscious of the flaming crimson that must be obvious on her own cheeks in the blistering sun, and her loose, messy ponytail next to the tidy chignon of her mother-in-law. She silently cursed herself for not washing her face and neatening up her hair before landing, but was also grateful for Nazar's garment selection. Left to her own devices she certainly would've selected a light skirt and blouse to travel in, and would've been embarrassed surrounded by the modest, elegant attire of her husband's family. She suddenly felt comfortable swathed in her black *abaya* in spite of the heat.

Ammi reached her hand out and took a lock of Mimi's strawberry blond hair between her fingers and said something to Nazar, a smile spreading across her face. Nazar answered her back in the language still foreign to Carolyn's ear, and Mimi lifted her head, turning to look at her new grandmother. The eyes of the two-year-old and the graceful woman locked on each other, and Ammi's façade softened.

"So sweet, *mashaAllah*," she said to Mimi, who reached her little hand up and curled her fingers around her grandmother's.

It was a touching moment Carolyn knew she would never forget. It became apparent that even if Ammi wasn't keen on having an American daughter-in-law, there would be no question of her finding a place in her heart for an American granddaughter.

A man who looked strikingly similar to Nazar emerged from behind his parents and clasped her husband's free hand. Iqra, who had been forgotten momentarily by Carolyn, whispered in her ear.

"That is my husband Safwat," she said. "Nazar's older brother."

Safwat turned to Carolyn with his eyes not quite meeting hers, made a bobbed bow, and said *salam*. He quickly turned back to his brother and the two carried on a rapid fire conversation with their parents nodding to whatever was being said. Ammi raised her slender arm

and snapped her fingers twice, and the entire entourage
began to move toward the building and out to the line of
cars waiting outside the busy airport.

"What about our bags?" Carolyn asked Nazar
when she realized they had left without them.

"The drivers know our names and have already
collected them," he replied.

She scanned the line of cars and spotted one
with their brand new canary yellow suitcase set tied to
the roof rack with heavy blue string. Mimi had picked
the luggage out shortly after they had obtained their
passports and Nazar wasn't thrilled when she came home
with the bright baggage, expecting a standard black suite
of bags. Carolyn had gone in with the same idea when
purchasing them, but once Mimi had locked her arms
around the smallest of the yellow cases, there was no
leaving the store without them.

Carolyn, Nazar, Mimi, and Ammi all squeezed
into the backseat of a sparkling black Mercedes Benz,
and Iqra slid into the front passenger seat beside the
driver. He was a stout brown man with engrained pox
scars scattered across his cheeks and bulbous nose. The
supple gray leather felt cool against Carolyn's back and
the interior had a heady, pleasant new car scent to it. The

driver turned on the ignition, and it took a moment for Carolyn to determine what was backward about the seating arrangement.

"Why is the driver's side on the right of the car and not the left?" she asked.

"Pakistan and India were British until the late forties," he answered, "so we don't follow the American driving side here. Not in the cars or on the roads."

Nazar lapsed into conversation with his mother and Iqra while Mimi dozed off on his lap. Carolyn looked out onto the dusty street as the driver jerked out into traffic onto what felt like the wrong side of the road. As they exited the airport and entered to the main road, the reality of where she had come to struck her. Dozens of people without the luxury of cars – let alone a Mercedes with a driver – walked along the sidewalks lugging the suitcases of family members they had met at the airport. The clothes for men seemed almost uniform: white, gray, or dusty brown tunic tops over flowing pants that tapered over the ankles. The *salwar kameez*, as Nazar had called them a hundred times, didn't look as strange when worn en mass by absolutely everyone. Women were clad in the same cut suits but in more colorful fabrics. What would've been vibrant colors were diluted with layers of dust over frocks exploding in bright floral and geometric patterns.

Along the sides of the roads were clusters of shops and houses in a higgly piggly setup without regard for design or structure. Dilapidated restaurants and shops sandwiched elegantly gated, stately homes and ramshackle houses with crumbling patched roofs that looked like they could collapse with a sneeze. With space at a premium, the shops were generally built up instead of out and from the top floors exposed open shutters with multihued laundry strung up to dry. Children played with sticks and the occasional coveted cricket bat out front of the buildings with little regard for traffic passing by.

The traffic itself was a mix of cars, rickshaws, and bicycles pouring into the streets, all honking their horns as if it signified anything but to move faster, or move at all. Carolyn couldn't help but chuckle to herself at Nazar comparing the driving customs of Lahore to those of Great Britain moments before. She had never been to England, but it appeared to her that Pakistani drivers had absolutely no rules for organized traffic whatsoever.

The car turned toward a gate, and a man in his late twenties leapt from a wooden dining chair behind it and heaved the gate open, allowing the car to pass onto an expanse of sandstone in front of a magnificent home.

"We're here," Nazar said.

As a child, Carolyn's mother had sometimes driven her through the more exclusive areas of San Francisco to look at homes that were so far beyond their reach that even make believing they could afford one was difficult. When she was able to catch a glimpse of a house beyond its layers of dense protective shrubbery and expensive gates, they occasionally resembled the home that stood before her now, even down to its muted pastel pink hue.

Four other cars pulled up and parked behind them, their doors opening and occupants flooding out. Abbu shouted something to the man in charge of the gate who hastily pulled it shut. One side of the heavy wood double door entry to the house swung inwards, and a matronly woman in a deeply faded burgundy *salwar kameez* and brown sandals emerged with a broom in her hand. She waved excitedly at Nazar with bright, happy eyes and a grin exposing a mostly toothless mouth.

"*Assalamualeikum,* Auntie Ji!" Nazar called to the woman, waving back to her.

"*Waleikumsalam,*" she replied, blushing as she approached the cars to help carry in lighter bags.

"She is your aunt Ji?" Carolyn asked, confused by the stark contrast in attire and grace between the woman and the rest of the ladies in Nazar's family.

"No," Nazar answered. "Auntie is what we call anyone older than us, really. Ji is just an added title as a sign of respect."

"That's kind of nice," Carolyn said. "But who is she actually?"

"She is a housekeeper who has worked for the family even before I was born. The guy at the gate, that's her son Aadil."

"What's her real name?"

"I…" Nazar thought for a moment. "You know, I've never asked that before. I have no idea what her name is." He shrugged his shoulders with indifference. "To be honest, even if I knew it I would never call her by her given name. It just isn't done."

"Where is her husband?" she pressed. "Where is Aadil's father?"

"Questions, questions!" Nazar laughed. "I don't know that either but Ammi would. Women don't discuss other women's personal lives with men, even their sons and husbands. If I had asked, Ammi probably would've just said he died, even if he didn't."

Carolyn looked at Aadil, who was assisting the driver in untying the luggage from the racks. Ammi took Nazar's arm and said something, gesturing towards the sleeping Mimi in his arms.

"C'mon," he continued, "let's get inside out of this sun."

They crossed through the doorway into the house, and Carolyn was rendered speechless. It was intended as nothing more than an entryway, but the white marble flooring and ornate sweeping staircase of the foyer took her breath away. They removed their shoes and followed Ammi and Iqra barefoot up the stairs. Carolyn allowed her hand to glide along the sandalwood banister and tilted her neck upwards to fully view the underbelly of an opulent crystal chandelier. They passed the second floor and made their way up to a third, where they were greeted by a two passages, the white marble continuing to stretch across the long expanses of both hallways. Carolyn continued to follow to the right, passing a doorway and coming to a second. Ammi turned the brass knob and pushed the door open.

"This is my room," Nazar whispered. "Our room."

Her breath caught in her throat. Her husband's childhood room was equal in size to all three bedrooms in their San Ramon condominium, with the addition of a large black and gold marbled ensuite bathroom.

Ammi and Nazar spoke to each other, and Iqra came to stand beside Carolyn.

"She is telling him to rest and then come down for dinner," Iqra confided.

"Yes, a bit of rest sounds wonderful," Carolyn said, the hours of travel and the burden of uncertainty at her welcome weighed heavily on her eyelids.

"She is also saying you and the child will need dresses," she continued before adding hesitantly, "but first, she needs to have a word with Nazar privately."

Carolyn went to her husband and lifted her daughter from his arms. Mimi stirred slightly before comfortably settling her head into the crook of Carolyn's neck.

"It's OK, Nazar," she said. "Go talk to your family."

He didn't argue with her and nodded before saying something back to his mother. Nazar left the room with Ammi and Iqra, closing the door softly behind them. Carolyn let out a heavy sigh and carried Mimi to the colossal mahogany Tudor style bed. It was fit for a king, queen, and all their many children. Together, mother and daughter collapsed easily onto the soft mattress and drifted off into a welcome slumber.

Chapter
12

The next few days were a whirlwind of fittings and fabric selection for Carolyn's *walima* dress. The tailor came to the house for the first time the morning after their arrival, and had returned once a day to fit scraps of cloth across Carolyn's body under Ammi's watchful eye.

Ammi's grasp of the English language was far superior to what Carolyn had initially believed based on the limited conversations the women shared. When talking to Nazar, Ammi always spoke in Urdu. Her chats with Mimi took on a much softer tone, and it was during these exchanges that Carolyn realized that Ammi was fluent in English and simply chose not to talk to Carolyn. Nazar did little to help her understand his mother's refusal to interact with her.

"We've been here four days, Nazar," she complained. "Your mom disappears with my daughter for hours at a time but refuses to talk to me. I know she speaks English. I've heard her with Mimi."

Nazar fingered a swatch of emerald green fabric, the color selected by Ammi for Carolyn's gown. "You aren't really making an effort yourself, Carolyn. All you do is stay in this room. Even Iqra is starting to give up on you."

Iqra had knocked on the door several times a day, offering Carolyn sweets and asking if she'd like to tour the city. She appreciated the kindness of her sister-in-law and her many attempts to draw her from the room, but was terrified of what lay beyond the house's safe gate and didn't have a taste for Pakistani treats. The flavor and textures were off. She had found Nazar's favorite, a coconut and pistachio *barfi*, to be chalky and live up to the American pronunciation of its name—

barfy. What she needed was Nazar to make her feel comfortable, and he spent all his time with his parents.

"It would be helpful if you made the effort on my behalf," she replied.

"Make the effort on your behalf?" he balked. "I can barely draw you out for meals. What am I supposed to do? Force you down the stairs?"

"Your mother won't talk to me, Nazar!" She flung her hands up to her head, rubbing her temples. "All of you are talking in Urdu. How do you think that makes me feel?"

"Urdu is the language we speak here, Carolyn! We're in Pakistan!" he shouted back. "This is my parents' house. They speak Urdu. They haven't seen me for years. What were you expecting?"

"Expecting? How could I possibly know what to expect when you didn't tell me anything." She pulled the bolt of fabric from his hand and waved it in front of his face. "I'm supposed to be the bride here. I sure don't feel like one."

"This isn't a wedding, Carolyn. This is a *walima*," he said. "We're doing this because it is *sunnah*."

"Oh yes," she replied. "*Sunnah*. Because all of the sudden you are so religious—getting up at the butt crack of dawn to pray and bowing up and down with your parents like you are such a good Muslim. It's a sham, Nazar. You don't pray at home. Now all the sudden you do it five times a day?"

His face turned red and he moved toward her. "You are a Muslim too, Carolyn. Remember? Remember saying *shahada* right before we married? I might not be a very good Muslim at home, but I will try harder in the future, and I will definitely do my bit here. I suggest you try to do the same."

"I don't even know how to pray!" she shouted. "And praying in Arabic, words I cannot even understand—I don't consider that prayer anyway."

"You don't—" he started, furious. He grabbed a fistful of his own hair into his hands and let out a load groan, unable to finish his sentence.

Carolyn had never seen him angry, and hadn't been so angry with him in all the time they'd been together. She felt isolated in a strange country where nobody seemed to like her, and now she had insulted her husband's faith.

Our faith, she thought.

"I shouldn't have said that," she admitted quietly. She had gone to Catholic masses and regurgitated prayers in Latin that were indecipherable to her at the time, but the strange words still moved her. In her heart they still felt like prayers. This wasn't any different. "I'm sorry, Nazar. I'm just floundering here."

His shoulders eased and he ran his fingers from the top of his head over his face, rubbing the exhaustion from his eyes. He released a sigh. "Are you a Muslim or not?"

The question hit her hard. How could he ask such a thing when he had never taught her what being a Muslim even was? Yes, she had said *shahada* before they married—but since then their lives hadn't changed a bit, except in giving up pork and alcohol. He didn't pray, or attend any mosque, or even fast during the month of Ramadan. They didn't celebrate either of the Eid holidays, which Carolyn only knew about because he casually mentioned the reasons for an extra call from his parents on those particular weeks.

"Are you?" she asked back. She didn't want to fight with him, but his question was a low blow.

"Yes, Carolyn, I am." He replied without hesitation. "I believe there is only one God, Allah, and that Muhammed is his final messenger. As I said, I may not be a very good Muslim. I might not practice as I should, but I still believe this in my heart." He looked at her, his soft eyes pleading for an answer. "Do you?"

"Yes," she answered, when in her heart she meant she didn't know. She wanted to learn, to try, for him. "I need to learn more. I can't be expected to understand things you have been taught from birth."

He nodded. "Let's start now. Let's pray together right now." He took her hand and gently led her into their bathroom, switching on the sink. "Before we pray, we have to do *wudu*. It's an ablution we do to clean our bodies of impurities before we pray."

He started by whispering *Bismillah* and washing both hands and wrists three times. He gargled water in his mouth and gently lifted a palm full of water to his nostrils. He washed his face, his forearms, and ran his wet hands across his forehead and to the back of his neck. He rubbed his earlobes and the back of his ears. Finally, he brought each foot under the running water and cleaned his feet, carefully wetting his ankles and scrubbing between his toes.

"Now you do it," he encouraged her.

Carolyn carefully repeated each of his actions three times, the water cooling against her warm skin and refreshing her body and spirit. The anxiety running down the drain with the used water.

He helped secure a headscarf over her hair, and then she stood to his right on a mat he'd laid out for her, copying his motions and movements as he said the prayers in Arabic. When she pressed her forehead to the floor during their first prostration, a tear released itself from her cheek and onto the soft rug.

From the doorway, Ammi peered in through a crack where the door had been left slightly ajar. She left the couple alone to finish their prayers and moved quietly down the hall, announcing to the family downstairs that it was time they tried to speak English when Carolyn was present.

Chapter 13

The *walima* was held at the family home, and Ammi had invited friends and members of the extended family to join in the celebrations. Guests were accommodated in tents around the house that had been draped in green and yellow garlands of fresh flowers. Silver trays of savory and sweet food were lined up and served to the hoards of guests by a wait staff Ammi had hired.

Carolyn's gown was stunning. Heavy beads of emerald green and gold across a chiffon so delicate she couldn't comprehend how it carried such a weight. Once her hair and make-up were completed by a highly regarded beautician, also arranged by Ammi, she stared at herself in the mirror in disbelief. She looked like herself, but a version so glamorous she could hardly recognize the reflection. The make-up was so thick she felt like she was wearing a mask. A deep line of kohl drawn across her eyes brought out their light color under a heavy lid of long, false eyelashes. It was astonishing— artistic—and she was grateful to know there was a professional photographer out in the tents to capture her in this moment. This was a look she would never be able to recreate, and she wanted to remember it always.

"You look like a dream," Nazar said as he entered the room. His eyes grew moist as he took her in.

"I feel like a porcelain doll," Carolyn replied. "You look great too. Is that a new suit?"

Nazar had foregone traditional Pakistani clothing and instead wore a black three-piece suit with a tie that matched Carolyn's gown. He looked amazing, but she definitely felt like the star of this show.

"It is." He smiled.

She walked to him and straightened his tie. "I know it hasn't been an easy trip, but I'm happy to be here. I'm happy to have a proper wedding reception."

"I'm just glad it all turned out all right." He kissed her lightly on the forehead.

Since their argument, there had been a drastic change in Ammi's conduct toward her. English was mostly spoken, and Carolyn finally started feeling a part of the family. There was still a nagging reservation in her belly about whether or not they truly accepted her, but by all appearances, they had certainly done their best. She was relieved they would be going home in two days and hoped that 7,500 miles was enough distance to keep the influence of her in-laws at bay. Nazar had continued to pray with her and the rest of the family five times a day, and had gone for Jummah prayers with his father and brother on Friday afternoons. It had been a nice bonding experience for her at first, but she grew tired of the continual ablution and prayer schedule quickly. She was ready to go home—but for tonight, she was ready to shine.

The party lasted until the early morning hours. Carolyn and Nazar were seated on a sea green velvet sofa atop an intricately decorated stage. Unlike a western wedding reception, the Asian version required little more than Carolyn smiling for photo after photo as guests lined up to take pictures with Nazar and his glowing *gori* wife.

"The guests are having all the fun," she pointed out to Nazar. "Do we have to sit here all night?"

"I'm afraid so," he said. "It's not so bad, is it?"

Carolyn laughed. "My cheeks hurt from all the smiling."

"Mimi's having a nice time." He peered around Carolyn to his mother and Mimi, who sat in a matching armchair just to the side.

Mimi could not be removed from Ammi's side. Carolyn had tried to call her daughter over, but the girl had been so spoiled by her grandmother that she refused to spend a few moments on her mother's lap.

"I'm terrified about how she will react when we leave." Carolyn had been nervous about the attachment. Mimi hadn't shown that degree of affection for anyone except herself and Nazar.

Nazar cleared his throat. "I don't want you to get angry because I obviously told her no, but Ammi asked if Mimi could stay behind with them. Learn the language and become a proper Muslim."

Carolyn swallowed hard. "You better tell me right now that you are joking, or I might scream."

"I'm joking," he said sternly. "Calm down."

"How could you joke like that?" she asked. The next group of family approaching the sofa for their turn with the couple and the photographer paused, and Carolyn realized she may have been speaking a little louder than she'd thought. She plastered a smile on her face and waved the hesitant group over with her hands.

A matronly woman dressed as decadently as Carolyn winked at her. Many of the younger ladies were wearing what appeared to be their own wedding dresses. In another opposing twist to the customs of the west, Carolyn quickly discovered that there was no similar unwritten rule in Pakistan that you do not try to outshine the bride. To Carolyn's well veiled disappointment, Iqra radiated above all the women present in both elegance and beauty, including herself. Carolyn couldn't fault her sister-in-law for anything. Iqra's loveliness radiated as brightly from the inside as it did across her face. It was difficult to not be slightly jealous.

"You...look...beauty," a woman said to Carolyn in broken English. "*MashaAllah.*"

Carolyn nodded a thank you to the stranger and stared into the flashing bulb of the camera. It was unbelievable that Ammi had so many friends. She could hardly believe this was all family. There was the usual exchange of polite words in Urdu between Ammi, Abbu, Nazar, and the group posing for the photo before they exited the stage and the next approached.

When the night began to transition into morning, Carolyn and Nazar were free to leave the stage and make their exit. Her stomach rumbled in protest to the morsels of sweets—sweets she didn't like—put in her mouth, and she ached for real food that she hadn't had time to enjoy. They entered the house together and made their way up the never-ending staircase to the bedroom, where Mimi had been long asleep in the bed. She ran her fingers across her daughter's face and kissed her on the cheek.

"You weren't joking earlier, were you?" she asked. "About Ammi asking Mimi to stay?"

Nazar unfastened his necktie. "No, but I told you I said she wouldn't."

Carolyn took a final look at herself in the mirror before she began to pull bobby pins from the silken *dupatta* that sat just behind her hairline. "I don't understand how anyone could even ask that."

153

"The intention was sincere," he replied. "Things are done differently here. People want better lives for their children, so they are willing to do whatever it takes to give them that."

Carolyn turned around from the mirror to face him. "And they think Mimi would have a better life here with them, separated her own mother?"

"If it was up to them you would stay too, Carolyn. We all would."

"But we aren't," she replied. "And that still doesn't answer why they would want to take my baby away."

"They don't want to take her away, Carolyn." He was becoming visibly frustrated again. "They just want to have her for a while. Let it go. She isn't staying, and I don't want to argue with you anymore."

Let it go. It was so hard for her not to take these things personally, and so easy for him to brush them aside. He couldn't see the insult through their concern. Worse, he defended it as if it were normal. The sickness in her stomach rose up again, and this time it wouldn't subside. She rushed to the toilet and heaved the sticky sweets from her stomach into the black porcelain bowl.

Barfy, indeed, she swore to herself silently.

Chapter
14

Within a few days of their return to San Ramon, Carolyn discovered the source of her stomach troubles had little to do with its disagreement to authentic Pakistani food. After a quick visit to the doctor expecting to be prescribed antibiotics for some form of Delhi Belly, Carolyn was pleasantly surprised to learn she was nine weeks pregnant. Nazar was thrilled when she told him, and immediately called Ammi to share the good news.

Nazar's younger brother Lut came to congratulate the couple on their marriage, not mentioning the pregnancy out of a sense of propriety. Nazar had been able to keep their relationship a secret in the early years, but that was no longer necessary after the *walima*. The secret was out, and they were free to live openly as a family.

Of the three brothers, Carolyn found Lut to be the most religious and, without a doubt, the most handsome. He stood slightly taller than Nazar and had striking features that looked more Hispanic in Carolyn's opinion than he did Pakistani. He was also a medical student, which heightened her esteem for him. More than once she had caught herself wondering if she had fallen for the wrong brother. It was a guilty joke she privately entertained in her mind.

Lut began to make regular visits, and Mimi reveled in the attentions of her new uncle, who was always up for a trip to the park or a game of hide and seek with her. Carolyn found him to be easy to talk to and wonderful company. While Nazar had reverted to his non-observant version of Islam, Lut seemed to lure it back out during visits and he would pray with Lut when he stopped by.

"Your brother, has he always been so devout?" Carolyn asked on an afternoon sunny enough for Lut to take Mimi to the playground.

"Not really," Nazar answered. "He became more so after moving here."

That didn't make any sense to her. "How would he become more so moving to a Christian country?"

"He really just stayed true to our upbringing. He found a mosque and went for prayers, and as he became more involved at the masjid and made friends, he just grew stronger in his faith." Nazar shrugged. "I don't really know. I don't talk to him about it much."

"Is Ammi sending him pictures of potential brides the way she did for you?" she teased.

"No, not for Lut. He's still in school, but the second he graduates and finishes his residency, he can expect an envelope of photographs all for himself." Nazar smiled at Carolyn.

The joking between them had been few and far between. It was nice to have a lightness in their banter, even if it was at Lut's expense. "Well, he's going to be quite the catch." She giggled.

"A doctor always is." Nazar replied.

"Yeah, but not just because he's a doctor. He's kind of hot too."

The smile disappeared from Nazar's face. Carolyn regretted the choice of words. "I mean for a Pakistani guy," she said, trying to back peddle. "He's as good looking as you. You two are both—"

"Please stop talking," Nazar interrupted. "I know what you meant, but I didn't need to hear it from my wife. Lut has always turned heads, the same way Iqra has."

It was like a punch in her stomach. Iqra. Beautiful, charming, dazzling, perfect, righteous Iqra. No doubt if Iqra had been intended for Nazar and not Safwat, Carolyn would be nothing more than mud under his happy foot. "Yes," she smiled. "Iqra is just lovely."

"Lut would never marry unislamically. Even if, Allah forbid, Ammi or Iqra weren't around to find him a wife, he'd still go through the traditional channels. He wouldn't date."

"He wouldn't do what you did," Carolyn said, knowing she was picking at his words, instigating a fight but unable to stop herself. "He wouldn't marry a silly American."

"He wouldn't marry a non-Muslim," he replied simply.

"As you did."

She had to get the jab in. She knew that wasn't what he meant, but jealousy boiled up inside of her. Jealousy of his relationship with his parents—that she never had with her own. Jealousy of Iqra and the perfection of tradition and culture she embodied—that Carolyn didn't have. Jealousy of Lut for, well, she didn't even know what—but whatever it was, it made her angry. In her mind everything was so backward in this family, but still—it made her feel something in her life had been lacking.

Nazar's face turned red and he started to leave the room shouting behind him, "Yes, Carolyn! Yes, yes, yes!"

She followed him into their bedroom. "Yes, yes, yes!" she repeated through gritted teeth. "You made a mistake, marrying a girl with a child! Admit it! You made a mistake!"

"I made no mistake," he seethed. "I love Mimi, and I care about you."

"You care about me, Nazar? You care about me?" She saw red, and her rage bubbled to the surface.

She raised her fists and pushed him as hard as she could, pressing into his back.

Nazar stumbled forward and caught himself on the dresser. She could see his back heaving and he turned around, raising his hand. She braced in anticipation for what was to come next, squeezing her eyes shut and cowering with her hands over her face.

He reached behind her with his raised hand and grabbed his jacket from the hook on the door. "I'm not going to hit you. I have more self control than you do." He stormed past her, leaving the apartment and slamming the door behind him.

She raced to the front door and reached it just as Lut came in with Mimi.

"What's going on?" he asked, genuine concern on his face.

Carolyn tried to move around him to get to her husband. To tell him she was sorry.

Lut blocked her. "Let him cool off," he said. "If you don't want to talk about it with me, that's fine, but let him cool off."

Carolyn collapsed on the floor and erupted into sobs. She reached up for Mimi, who sat bewildered in her uncle's arms. Lut lowered his niece to her, and

Carolyn took the little girl to her chest, rocking back and forth and burying her face in her daughter's soft curls.

"Can I get you something?" Lut asked softly. "Are you OK?"

"I'll be fine," she whispered. Mimi wrapped her arms around Carolyn's neck, patting her little hands against her mother's hair. She kissed her daughter on the cheek and stood up to face Lut. "I think I'm losing my mind," she said.

"We all do it sometimes," he replied, smiling. "You want to talk about it?"

Carolyn shook her head. Lut was the last person she wanted to know she had become violent with her own husband—his brother.

He didn't press her, and instead picked up a pencil and turned over a white envelope on the counter. He scrawled what looked like a phone number on it, but it had way too many digits for that to be what it was.

"This is Ammi's phone number in Pakistan," he said. "If there are problems it's good to have someone in the family to talk to. And she wants what is best for you."

Carolyn looked at the paper. "I don't think she'd want to talk to me, Lut."

He pushed the paper to her again. "You're wrong," he said. "She would want to help if she can."

Carolyn picked up the paper and tucked it into her pocket. She was grateful for Lut's concern, but there was only one place she felt she could go to feel at peace.

"I think I'm going to go for a walk with Mimi," she said.

"Call her, Carolyn," he pressed, "for anything at all. She wants you both to be happy, as we all do."

"With all due respect, I don't think Ammi is the best person to talk to about my marriage."

He smiled. "With all due respect, I think she is. Call her for anything."

Lut encouraged her to call Ammi once more before leaving. Once he was gone, Carolyn readjusted Mimi's little coat and then wrapped herself in her own. There was only one place where she thought she could find peace. It was the peace she found as a child, not knowing what provided it, only that she felt its embrace. It was a bit of a walk, and Mimi had fallen asleep by the time she rolled the stroller in front of tan brick building. A metal, life-sized sculpture of a woman on a horse lifting her sword towards the sky stood before the door,

and Carolyn entered the sanctuary she had sought out:
The Saint Joan of Arc Catholic Parish.

Most Beloved

The Prophet Muhammad (pbuh) grew up in his loving uncle's house, blossoming into a youth of exceptionally good character, marking him out from the rest of the young Makkans. He soon began to assist Abu Talib - leader of the Banu Hashim clan - in trade and commerce, further revealing his talents and integrity. His honesty and reputation preceded him and sometime after his return to Makkah from Syria, he took up a trading job with one of the wealthiest and noblest Quraishite women, Khadija (RA). Khadija (RA) entrusted him with money, with which he busied himself in commerce. He travelled back to Syria and made great profits for Khadija (RA) during the trip. Naturally, Khadija (RA) was pleased and soon came to admire Muhammad's (pbuh) intelligence and honesty, in time wanting to offer her hand in marriage to him.

So, she sent her sister to this young man. She asked him, "Why are you not married, yet?"

"For lack of means," he answered.

"What if I could offer you a wife of nobility, beauty, and wealth? Would you be interested?" she told him.

He replied in the affirmative, but when she mentioned her sister, the young employee chuckled in amazement.

"How could I marry her? She has turned down the most noble men in the city, much wealthier and prominent than me, a poor shepherd," he said.

"Don't you worry," the sister replied, "I'll take care of it."

Muhammad (pbuh) married Khadija (RA) and they lived a harmonious life full of love and sincerity, sharing each other's joys and sorrows. They formed a perfect husband and wife pair, the likeness of which is something rare in human history. Khadijah (RA) was a source of immense love, strength, and comfort for the Prophet Muhammad (pbuh), and he leaned heavily on this love and support on the most important night of his life.

When the Divine Message of the Holy Quran was revealed to Muhammad (pbuh), the devout Khadija (RA) at once believed in her husband without ever expressing the slightest doubt. She was the first among women to accept Islam and subsequently put all her vast wealth and property at the Prophet's disposal for the spread of truth and justice. She endured with him hunger, poverty, and the calamities inflicted upon Muslims by the Makkans who did not accept Islam. When the Prophet Muhammad (pbuh) and his family was banished to the hills outside of Makkah, she went there with him, and the years of hardship and deprivation eventually led to her death.

In the tenth year of the Prophetic mission, Khadija (RA) breathed her last breath. It was a great tragedy for the Prophet. The year is known as the 'Year of Grief' in history and even in later years of his life after numerous marriages, he used to cherish her loving memory and refer to her as the most beloved of his spouses. Once, years after Khadijah (RA) died, he came across a necklace that she once wore. When he saw it, he remembered her and began to cry and mourn. His love for her never died, so much so, that his later wife Ayesha (RA) once she asked if Khadijah (RA) had been the only woman worthy of his love. The Prophet replied:

"She believed in me when no one else did; she accepted Islam when people rejected me; and she helped and comforted me when there was no one else to lend me a helping hand."

Ivy
1985 - Tampa, Florida

Ivy reset her watch to California time as she stepped off the flight from Florida and made her way through the airport terminal with a roller bag too large to have been allowed as carry on. Her heart was pounding, and the butterflies in her stomach were making her regret opting for the heavy beef meal she had chosen on the flight over the lighter fish option. She had spoken to Lut on the phone many times in the past four months, but meeting the man for the first time was an altogether different game. Thankfully, she'd told him that she'd call from the hotel and meet him for dinner so there'd be time for her to clean up and collect herself beforehand.

Having never been through Oakland airport before, she was relieved to spot a man in a smart gray suit holding a sign with her name on it.

"I'm Ivy McAdams," she said to the driver.

He smiled and reached to take her bag from her, bright white teeth like reflectors against his ebony skin. "Well hello there, Ms. McAdams! I'm your driver Leroy. Welcome to the bay."

Ivy smiled back and allowed his open friendliness swallow up some of her nervousness.

"We're taking you to the Sir Francis Drake Hotel in the city today?" he asked, still grinning.

"That is correct," Ivy replied. "Do you know how to get there?"

"Ms. McAdams," he said with a laugh so robust it must have come from the depths of his belly, "everybody knows where the Sir Francis Drake is!"

Ivy couldn't help but chuckle at the Leroy's pleasantness. "I had been warned San Francisco could be quite unfriendly," she joked, "but you're certainly proving the stereotype wrong."

"Well you're still in Oakland!" he teased.

Ivy cringed slightly. She'd heard even more unpleasant things about Oakland. Her younger sister Josie had graduated from San Francisco State three years before and immediately moved back to Tampa. Josie loved San Francisco as a whole but had frequently bemoaned its affluence. The few times she had mentioned Oakland, it was as its polar opposite.

"It's all just people not really knowing either place very well," he assured her with a sincere smile. "San Francisco can be uppity, and Oakland is a bit more real – but both cities are gems. You're going to have a real nice time. C'mon now," he continued, "let's get you to that fancy hotel of yours!"

Once in the Lincoln Town Car, Leroy's friendly demeanor carried on with easy conversation that further relaxed Ivy.

"So what brings you to San Francisco, Ms. McAdams?" he asked.

"I'm actually here to meet someone," she replied tentatively, not sure how to explain such an unconventional meeting to a stranger – no matter how nice the stranger was.

"A friend?" he pressed.

"Yes, a friend." A friend. A boyfriend. A potential fiancé. She wasn't even sure herself what to call him.

Leroy's ease and experienced driving had them in front of the Sir Francis Drake in under an hour. Her bag was passed from her driver to a friendly doorman dressed in a long, bright scarlet Elizabethan velvet frock coat, knee-high socks, and Beefeater's hat. Thanking Leroy, she tipped him generously and confirmed her return pick-up in five days before entering the hotel.

She took her key to the sixteenth floor and was glad when she entered her room that she had treated herself to a suite. The room was spread out like a kitchenless apartment with a sizeable living room and separate bedroom, both with views that overlooked Union Square. She wanted a place where she and Lut might be able to sit and chat without a bed in the middle that could insinuate a progression in the relationship that might be uncomfortable. She couldn't be sure that the chemistry from their phone conversations and letters would not be absent in person. No need to make an prickly situation worse. For tonight, they were meeting upstairs on the twenty-first floor for alcohol-free cocktails – mocktails, as he called them - at the Starlight Room.

She picked up the phone next to the plush, black velvet sofa and dialed his number. It was ingrained in her memory, but this was the first time she felt nervous calling him in the four months they had been talking.

"Hi Lut," she said slowly when he answered. "It's Ivy."

"Ivy!You're here now?"

"I just checked in. When do you want to meet?"

"Four months ago!" he answered, laughing. "I can be there in two hours, so around seven?"

"Seven is perfect," she said. It would give her enough time to shower and get ready for what felt like the biggest interview of her life.

"I can't believe I am finally going to get to see you face to face," he said. "I'm really excited."

"Me too," she admitted. "So I will see you at the Starlight Room at seven."

"See you then, Ivy."

"Bye."

She returned the handset into the cradle and let out a sigh. Four months. Four months of phone calls and letters. Four months of flirtation and sharing each other's intimate secrets. Four months of working toward this moment, deciding once and for all if it was going to end tonight or last forever. He has been clear from the beginning. He wasn't looking for a girlfriend, and he didn't date. He was a Muslim man, and he was looking for a wife. He was looking for her, and after years of failed relationships, at the age of 27, she was certainly looking for him.

To the shock and poorly concealed horror of her Christian family, Ivy had said *Shahada* and become a Muslim the year before. Her previous boyfriend Altaf was an American-born Iraqi, a non-practicing Muslim in a family of devotees. Ivy had befriended Altaf's older sister Amina, who had ulterior motives and formed the friendship to try and reform her young brother's white girlfriend in the hopes of reforming her feral brother. Amina began bringing Ivy to *hadeeth* and *tawheed* classes for women in the evenings at her Tampa masjid, explaining to her why a dating relationship was *haram* – forbidden – and what Ivy would have to morph it into for it to be *halal* – permissible. Initially Ivy went hoping to secure the favor of her boyfriend's sister, but as the classes continued and her knowledge of Islam developed, she quickly decided that Altaf was not a man she could see her future with and ended the relationship. Having lost her ally, Amina stopped attending the classes while Ivy became more involved, adding Quran classes to her repertoire of lessons and eventually becoming a Muslim herself. She leaned heavily on her dearest childhood friend Safia, a born Muslim, as she began to transition her lifestyle and grow in her *deen*.

The introduction between Ivy and Lut had been simple and almost too good to be true. Safia had come to San Francisco for a wedding and had reconnected with Lut at the nuptials of their mutual college friend. Safia and Lut hadn't seen each other for four years but she remembered him as a studious, hardworking, and wildly attractive man. Happily engaged herself, Safia didn't think much of Lut until he casually mentioned that his mother was pressing him to get married.

As their conversation progressed, Lut revealed his reservations about marrying a home-grown Pakistani bride, worried about her easily adapting to American culture. He didn't see himself moving back to Lahore in the next ten years, if at all. A light clicked in Safia's head, and she gave Ivy's phone number to Lut, describing her as a new revert to Islam who was also looking to settle down. Lut called Ivy a few days later, and they had been courting ever since.

Ivy unclasped the oversized belt buckle at her waist and slipped out of her pantsuit. She inspected her naked body in the bathroom's full-length mirror, turning from side to side. Anticipating the meeting, she had spent her mornings over the past five weeks dedicated to home aerobic workouts and a super low-calorie diet. Her dedication paid off, and she had quickly transformed her soft, plump frame into a firmer, smaller version of herself. Ivy knew it was a short-term solution and, like all the times before, her naturally round figure would fight its way back to a comfortable, fleshier weight. The knowledge of this did little to diminish her appreciation of the form reflected back in the glass before her. Giving herself a final smile and twist of the hips, she stepped into the shower and began to meticulously shave, scrub, and groom herself.

Ivy had selected a white lace top lined with black nylon and a tea-length black taffeta skirt for her first meeting. The black sash that sat high on the waist elegantly accentuated her slender form without any emphasis to her heavy bosom and backside, which she intentionally concealed. The boxy trends of the day had made dressing fashionably modest surprisingly easy, and she was grateful for it. Still possessed with a degree of vanity, she wasn't ready for an *abaya* and headscarf except at the masjid. Safia had encouraged baby steps in Ivy's personal evolution into Islam, noting that it was more important that she take on more as it became comfortable as opposed to jumping in head first only to drown later.

She pulled the giant rollers from her dark brown hair and finished her lips off with a coat of clear lip gloss. The result was striking and her nerves settled with a fresh dose of self confidence.

"I would marry me," she said, giggling to herself in the mirror before skipping out the door.

They couldn't have picked a quieter night to go to the popular nightspot sitting on top of the historic building. When Ivy walked in and was greeted by the host, she immediately spotted Lut through the crimson red drapes at a table for two by the window. He stood quickly as he watched her enter, knocking a napkin and drink card onto the floor. He looked even better in person than he had in the few photos he had sent her, although slightly shorter. A broad smile lit up his lightly bronzed face.

"Is that really you?" he asked as she approached, holding out both his hands.

She placed her own into his palms and her heart fluttered in her chest. "It's really me," she said, elated.

"You are stunning," he said sincerely.

Her hands grew warm at his touch and she pulled them back slowly, moving towards the rich taupe chair and settling into it. "Thank you," she said softly.

Neither could stop smiling, and in her mind Ivy was praising Allah to the moon and back for sending her such a beautiful man.

"I ordered us virgin Mojitos," he said, bending over to collect the napkin and card from the floor. "You said mint was your favorite, so I guessed it would be all right."

"It's perfect," she replied.

The silence as they took each other in was unusually comfortable. They sat staring at each other, almost as old friends meeting after a long period of separation. Their conversations had covered religion and past relationships, family histories and stories, expectations, and hopes for the future. In a brief span of time and without the distraction of a physical relationship, their correspondence and talks had created a relationship founded firmly on honesty and openness. Had they been dating, the physical bond may have overpowered the need to dig deeper emotionally as it had in Ivy's previous romances. This was different. This was reversing the way a relationship normally progressed, starting with an explicit understanding that they were getting to know one another for a single purpose: matrimony. It fell outside the boundaries of what Muslims believed to be appropriate – meeting privately and arranging it independently – but it was still a refreshingly old-fashioned method in Ivy's eyes.

The drinks arrived and were placed in front of them. Ivy lifted her glass and took a sip of her mocktail. She hadn't realized how dry her mouth had become until it was hit by the minty limeade.

"My family thinks I am crazy," she said. "My mom asked if it was safe, flying across the country to meet my pen pal."

Lut laughed, choking on his mojito. "She thinks I'm just a pen pal? That's funny!"

"She knows you aren't, but she calls you that anyway for lack of a better description."

"My brother knows I am here, but he didn't think it was a great idea."

They had spoken before at length on his brother Nazar's marriage to an American woman. He hadn't elaborated – saying it was unislamic to back bite – but she knew the marriage wasn't a harmonious one. He had mostly talked about his love for his adopted niece Mimi and nephew, Adam.

"How far away from you do they live?" she asked.

"Less than forty minutes," he answered. "When I first came to America, Nazar and I lived together, but when he bought the gas station I started medical school, and the commute to Palo Alto was impossible." He took another sip from his drink. They had this conversation several times before but Ivy liked hearing about his city hopping, having only ever lived in Tampa. "When I graduated I did my residency in Berkeley and have lived there ever since."

"Would it be hard to move away?" she asked, wishing she hadn't asked the question as soon as it came out of her mouth. "I mean to say, if –"

"It won't be hard to move away," he reassured her, moving his hand across the table to hold hers. "It definitely won't be hard to move away."

He spoke with such firmness that Ivy blushed. They had discussed her reservations about leaving her family to move cross country and, even though her advertising job was less grand than his work as a doctor, she was close to her parents, and his were thousands of miles away. She didn't want to leave Florida, and he knew that. They had decided early on that it would be he that moved should "everything work out" between them.

Did his answer mean everything was working out? Her cheeks turned even brighter red.

"Well?" Lut asked.

"Well what?" she replied, almost whispering. Please, please let it be what I think -

"Shall we get a *nikkah*?" he proceeded cautiously. "Shall we get married?"

Ivy sat speechless for a moment. She had hoped it would come this easily but certainly wasn't expecting him to advance to the subject within the first ten minutes of seeing each other. But she knew him, truly, and he knew her. This is what they had planned all along, and it felt right. It was right.

"We shall," she said, her heart flooding over with joy.

Chapter
16

Before she left, Safia had helped Ivy pick out a
simple white chiffon *abaya* that wrapped loosely around
her body with velvet trim and a flattering empire waist.
Her headscarf, which she knew she would need for the
straightforward Islamic signing of the wedding contract
– the *nikkah* – was matched and trimmed perfectly. They
would have a legal, civil ceremony back in Florida
where she could wear the traditional wedding dress her

mother would want, but for this one, the one that meant the most to both of them, simple elegance was what she was striving for. She was grateful her friend Safia had the foresight to predict Lut would want to get married right away, and even more so that the hotel was able to press the dress with little more than a few hours notice.

The night before had ended quite early, with Lut planting a chaste kiss on her fingertips and telling her he would call the next morning to let her know the details. He told her to be prepared, because they would definitely be getting a *nikkah* the next day. True to his word, he called her at ten to let her know he would be at the hotel room that afternoon with an Imam, his brother, his sister in law, and the Imam her own masjid in Florida had contacted on short notice to act as her *wali* – her guardian.

"It is only seven in Florida!" she exclaimed. "How on earth did you get in touch with them to arrange a *wali* of their choosing?" She was completely perplexed. It didn't even seem possible.

"I called Safia last night, and she managed the whole thing," he replied.

He had called her best friend and told her they were getting married before she did. She felt a lump grow in her throat. She was in such a state of bliss the whole night she had only called her sister, who didn't answer. She was ashamed to have not considered the very friend who picked out her gown and talked her through the whole process as a just-in-case before she boarded the plane.

"The Imam at your mosque is responsible for you since you do not have any Muslim relatives," he continued, unaware of her distress. "Her father was able to reach someone last night, and an Imam from a masjid with ties to yours is available to be your *wali* today."

"I would've preferred to talk to someone from my masjid myself, Lut. Or at least speak to Safia first." She tried to keep the concern from her voice and bear in mind that he was doing exactly what should be done, but it still hurt that he had completely left her out of it.

"Ivy," he said in a soft voice, all excitement drained. "Do you want to postpone this? Would you feel better doing it another day, doing it your way? Because I would understand if you did. It really would be OK."

Her heart sank. He sounded completely deflated, like she had sucked all the air out of a balloon. And it certainly wasn't what she wanted either. "No, Lut," she replied earnestly, "I definitely want to marry you today. Definitely."

Lut sighed heavily into the phone. "Oh, thank goodness!" he said, his excitement restored. "We'll be there at three!"

They hung up, and Ivy couldn't help but laugh. What bride has less than five hours notice for her own wedding, a wedding planned entirely by the groom? Lucky for her the dress was ready, her hair would be neatly secured under a scarf and without need of styling, and make-up was unusual beyond a light powdering and mascara for such a simple, religious ceremony. A simple, religious ceremony that tied her for the rest of her life to a man she had talked to for four short months and seen for all of an hour. It didn't matter. Ivy was in love.

The ceremony was short and sweet, as Ivy had anticipated. Her *wali*, a tall, lanky man from Peshawar, an uncle of Safia's, took his job as seriously as any father would. He brought his wife Zara along and before they proceeded, the couple spoke to Ivy quietly in the corner to ensure she was certain of her decision and to go over the terms of the contract, which they had translated to English for her benefit.

Lut's brother Nazar and Nazar's wife Carolyn were also in attendance, providing the necessary two male witnesses between Ivy's *wali* Baseem and Lut's older sibling. Carolyn was polite and friendly, but surprised Ivy slightly at the sight of a small gold cross around her neck. Lut had described her as a Muslim, having said *shahada* before marrying Nazar, but the cross spoke to the contrary.

Noticeably absent were the couple's two children, Lut's beloved niece and nephew. Ivy had hoped to meet them, but her disappointment soon vanished when the nuptials began. The room might as well have been empty except for her and Lut, for all her excitement in the moment.

The Imam from Lut's masjid was clearly someone who he held in high regard and knew well. He maintained a serious tone throughout the execution of the contract, but continually placed his hand on Lut's shoulder in a show of solidarity and paternal support. Zara held Ivy's hand, and Baseem stood protectively to her right, answering questions on her behalf as Zara squeezed Ivy's fingers with each acknowledgment. It was evident even in the absence of the bride and groom's biological parents, they were both represented by men who had their best interests at heart.

"It's lovely to finally meet you," Ivy said to Carolyn while the men and Zara talked amongst themselves after the signing.

"You as well." Carolyn smiled back at Ivy. "Although I'm sorry to admit I only heard about you a couple of days ago."

Ivy's heart sunk in her chest. She knew Lut was a fiercely private man, and that she was still unknown to his parents, but she had assumed that he had at least told his older brother and wife about her. She forged a strong grin across her face. "He's full of sercrets, that husband of mine."

"He sure is," Carolyn replied. She fingered the cross at her neck and looked Ivy square in the eye. "How long have you been Muslim?"

"Less than a year. My *wali* is uncle to a friend of mine back home."

"Does your family know you've gotten married?" She absentmindedly slid the cross back and forth across the delicate gold chain.

"They knew I might have a religious ceremony but are more interested in the white wedding we'll have in Florida." Ivy ran her fingers over the silky sleeve of her *abaya*, having forgotten this was technically a white wedding too. "I mean, the kind they are used to," Ivy laughed.

"What do they think," she asked, waving her hand in front of Ivy's dress and up towards her headscarf, "of all this."

"I haven't started wearing *hijab* at home," she admitted, "but I will soon, *inshaAllah*. They are confused about everything but accept me however I am."

Caroyln nodded in a *yes* motion. "Good," she replied simply.

Ivy struggled to decide whether or not her new sister-in-law was supportive of the marriage, or if this was all some sort of veiled condescension. Her smile was sincere, and the questions were what she'd consider normal between two white women married to Pakistani brothers, but her body language hinted at something gloomier that Ivy couldn't quite come to terms with.

After a lunch spread of fresh San Francisco seafood delivered on elegantly appointed tables rolled in by the hotel's room service, the Imams, Zara, Carolyn and Nazar said their goodbyes to the newly married couple. Nazar and Ivy were left alone in the lavish suite.

Ivy unpinned her headscarf and pulled it back off her forehead, allowing her hair to tumble freely around her shoulders. She had yet to kiss her husband, so the idea of spending the next night with him – an intimacy she had never shared with any man – made her skin prickle in excitement.

She massaged her scalp lightly as Lut came over to her. Placing one hand on her cheek and the other at her waist, he lowered his mouth gently over Ivy's. She kissed him back, an openmouthed invitation that he hungrily accepted.

"To the bedroom?" he whispered into her ear.
"Yes."

Her lack of experience seemed to excite him, but his love remained attentive and gentle. Even in the midst of his need she felt the tenderness in his restraint. When he finally entered her, she gasped, the initial jolt of pain quickly soothed by his reassuring whisper in her ear. His whispering became louder, his breath desperate and ragged. She moved with him, the warmth of his body encouraging her own to its climax. When he had spent himself inside of her, he ran his mouth along her jawbone until it found her earlobe.

"*Alhamdulillah* for you," he whispered. "*Alhamdulillah* for everything."

Chapter
17

Ivy returned home to Tampa and within two short weeks, at Lut's insistence, found a beach-front townhouse in the small city of Indian Rocks Beach. Lut had been hired as a general practitioner at a nearby Largo hospital and had stayed behind in Berkeley to finalize the sale of his condo and work through his final weeks at his Bay Area hospital. Ivy's concerns about the affordability such a luxurious home in a popular tourist hub were put to rest when Lut disclosed his respectable financial state to her prior to her departure from their San Francisco hotel.

The townhouse was less than thirty miles from her parents and sister in Tampa. Despite reservations they had at their daughter's method of obtaining a husband, they continued to support her in the decision and had gone with her to meet the real estate agent in front of the home to collect the keys.

"How can he afford this?" Ivy's mother asked as they walked through the entryway into a light blue and stainless nautical-themed kitchen.

"He's got a great job, Dorothy," her father replied, slapping his hand down on the cream granite countertop.

"Yes, but even so –" she trailed off as she wandered through into the oversized living room, making her way to a sliding glass door. She stared out at the sand just beyond the outdoor patio. "This is a rich man's vacation home, Jim."

"Isn't it beautiful?" Ivy asked, desperate for her mother's approval.

"It's breathtaking." she replied.

They stood together, quietly watching the ocean waves stroke the white sand. Ivy had previously counted two hundred and ten footsteps from her patio to the waterfront when she first saw the house. Two hundred and ten short strides to soak her feet in the warm salt water.

"It's still affordable even with you quitting your job?"

"Lut makes enough, Mom. Stop worrying."

"It's just so much change all at once, Ivy." Her mother released a sigh. "I'm concerned about it."

"Is it so strange Mom, Lut wanting to provide for his new bride and for me to settle in as a housewife? You're a housewife yourself. I have nothing but the greatest respect for how you devoted your life to your family."

"I wasn't educated, Ivy. I don't regret a second of it and wouldn't have it any other way, but I've always been proud of my girl's education and the career opportunities it has given you. We saved our entire lives to ensure both you and Josie got degrees. We did that to put you on the path to independence."

"I am independent," Ivy answered gently, "and an education opened up my world to more than just a job. I don't need to be selling advertising to assert my independence. I am independent because I have the freedom to think for myself. To make these decisions for myself."

"But did you make this decision yourself? It seems so strange, leaving your job to tend a home. If you had done it with a child on the way I could understand it, but not just to take care of a husband."

"Hey now!" Ivy's father interceded. "Nothing wrong with a woman taking care of her husband!" He wrapped his arms around her waist and kissed her shoulder. "She'll be good at it, like her mama is."

"Jim!" She giggled. "Stop being silly."

"I'm not being silly! Our daughter married a well-paid doctor, and now she can spend her free time doing what she likes, not what must be done to keep the power bill paid." He winked at Ivy. "And she likes visiting her parents."

Ivy laughed out loud and put her hand on her mother's arm. "Come see the rest of the house," she said. "There are three bedrooms upstairs and a wonderful balcony with a sea view from the master."

"You'll be cutting into your parent-visiting time decorating this place," her father joked.

"Not really." Ivy smiled. "I fully expect Mom's help."

Her mother's eyes lit up. "Oh, now you're just trying to butter up a cranky old lady!"

"We'll see about that," Ivy replied. "We might not have the same taste, but I definitely need your help. I don't even know where to start."

"I do," her mom said, a grin spreading across her face. "I only need to know one thing."

"What's that, Mom?"

"How much do we have to spend?"

Chapter
18

The day Lut finally moved to Florida was the happiest Ivy could recall, excluding their *nikkah* five weeks before. She had wanted to visit him in Berkeley, but he had insisted his hours at the hospital would be too long for him to give her the attention she deserved and desired. Instead, she filled her five-week wait decorating their new home and planning their simple civil ceremony. Her parents and sister had yet to meet Lut, and because of the unconventional nature of their courtship and marriage – by western standards, at least – they had all agreed a small family affair would be the best way to do it.

In the same style that Lut had surprised her with just a few hours notice of their wedding in San Francisco, Ivy had fired back with equal enthusiasm allowing roughly the same amount of time for their legal ceremony.

"Welcome home," she cried as they walked through the front door. Lut unceremoniously dumped his luggage in the hall.

"That was a long, long flight," he said, comfortable now in the privacy of their own house to grab her around the hips and kiss her.

"You have to see this place," she whispered against his lips.

"I only want to see one thing right now," he gently replied, "and that is you out of these clothes."

The chemistry between them had been undeniable and excruciatingly short. Ivy had been as sad to part from Lut and their San Francisco honeymoon suite as any bride might have. The letters and telephone conversations prior to their meeting had been strictly G-rated, whereas the days spent in bed following their wedding were anything but. When she returned to Florida, despite his exhaustion at working such long hours, their nightly phone calls had carried on in the spirit of their lusty holiday. She found herself blushing frequently the morning after a call, their explicit sex talk still dancing around in her mind.

"I want that too," she admitted. Ivy drew away from him slightly and took a step towards the stairs, but Lut grabbed her wrist and pulled her close again.

"No time for that," he murmured, lifting her up onto the kitchen countertop.

The sex was fast and frantic, a desperate jumble of heavy panting and rocking limbs. When it was over, Lut buried his forehead into Ivy's heaving chest and chuckled lightly.

"Your husband, Mister Romance," he teased.

Ivy tilted her head back and laughed softly, her throat still hoarse and struggling to catch an even breath. "Most men carry new brides across the doorway, not lift them onto a kitchen counter."

"Is that so, Mrs. Miah?" he asked, grinning. He looped his finger through a leg hole of the white cotton underpants that only made it off one of her ankles. "Well, put these back on and we can try again."

"You can do it tomorrow morning when I have on a puffy white dress!"

"Oh God, no-" he joked, "please tell me you did not get one of those American monstrosities!"

"I did! And when I have it on you are going to say you love it, even if you don't."

"I love you," he said, still flashing a set of even, white teeth. "Even if you dress like a marshmallow."

"I love you too," she said. "More than anything in the world."

The next morning came with a loud knock at the door. Ivy had been up since sunrise cooking for their wedding feast in three hours time, leaving Lut alone in the giant four poster cherrywood bed. She wiped her hands and opened the front door.

"Are we too early?" her father asked, his arms loaded with presents.

Her mother pushed past him carrying Ivy's freshly pressed wedding gown. "I picked up your dress."

"Thanks Mom," Ivy said. "You're right on time Dad."

He unloaded the gifts onto their white dining table. "Some loot for the bride and groom."

Ivy looked at the mound, surprised. "You didn't have to get us anything. Mom already stocked this house with more gadgets than I'll ever need."

"Oh shush," her mother replied. "There were some small things we didn't get that I remembered after."

"Where's my new son-in-law?" her father asked, looking around as if Lut might spring from one of their oak cabinets.

As if on cue, Lut came down the stairs in a pair of sweatpants and a blue polo shirt.

"Here he is," Lut said smiling. He extended his hand to her dad, who brushed his hand away and went in for one of his famous bear hugs.

"None of that now, you hear?"

The towering frame of Ivy's father practically swallowed her shorter husband up.

"Jim!" her mom cried. "You're going to scare the poor boy off!"

He released Lut and gave him a heavy handed pat on the back. "We're a huggin' family."

Ivy's mother approached the men and gave Lut a peck on each cheek, leaving a smudge of coral lipstick on both sides of his face. "We're so glad you're here, honey."

From behind her mother's back, Ivy winked at Lut and voicelessly mouthed, "Sorry."

"Where's Josie?" Ivy asked. She had expected her sister to arrive with the dress hours before her parents.

"She's on her way," her mom replied. "Any minute now, she'll be here."

"So what's the plan today?" her father asked. He walked over through the living room to the sliding glass door. "It's a beautiful day for a beach wedding."

"The officiant will be here in two hours," Ivy answered. "It'll just be the four of us, Josie, and Safia."

"Why are you making so much food, then?" her dad asked. All four stove burners were bubbling away, and the oven had been working overtime.

"Give it a rest, Jim," her mom said. "You know how much Ivy Girl loves to cook."

"A damn fine cook she is, too" he said, quickly looking to Lut. "Sorry. Didn't mean to use the D word."

Lut put up his hand in a gesture of politeness. "Don't apologize on my account. I can handle the D word."

All four laughed together. "See," he dad bellowed. "We're bonding already!"

"You two boys are going to have to ske-daddle," her mom said, still giggling. "I know you are already married according to Him," she pointed toward the heavens, "but I still think it's bad luck to see your bride on your wedding day. You're already pushing it. Ivy, honey. You should've stayed at our house last night."

Ivy felt herself blush as she remembered how they had spent the night before—and the earliest hours of the morning.

"Shall we go out for a breakfast of our own, Mr. McAdams?" Lut asked his father-in-law.

"Mr. McAdams?" he scoffed. "I hope you don't think I'm going to allow you to call me that! It's Jim. Just Jim. But yes," he continued, "let's leave the ladies to their girly things."

He made a move towards the door, and Ivy met Lut's eyes. She knew he never left the house after sex without showering first, and they had enjoyed each other right after praying Fajr together at sunrise. Cleanliness is half of faith. The Prophet himself, peace and blessings be upon him, had said that.

"I need Lut to shower first, Dad," she said. "In case we are running behind. Then he can just put on his suit and meet us on the sand. It also leaves the bedroom free for me to get ready later."

"I'll only be a minute," Lut said. He hurried up the stairs, bounding two steps at a time.

"Such a beautiful man he is," her mom whispered quietly to Ivy. "Quite the looker."

"He's beautiful on the inside too, Mom."

True to his word, Lut was back down in under five minutes wearing a fresh pair of jeans and a crisp white dress shirt. The two men left the house together and allowed mother and daughter to spend some time alone preparing before the intimate gathering. It was, and her father had said, a beautiful day for a wedding. A picnic table had been moved to the patio, and they busied themselves covering it with ivory linen and Ivy's new Royal Doulton fine bone china place settings. Two bottles of sparkling cider were positioned on ice in their own silver champagne buckets. She was relieved her parents didn't seem to notice or care that they wouldn't be toasting the couple with alcohol.

Josie arrived with their two-tiered white wedding cake and Safia just a few minutes later with Ivy's dusty pink tea rose and lily bridal bouquet.

"Something borrowed and something blue," Safia said as she handed the fresh flowers to Ivy, pointing to a powder blue ribbon securing the stems together.

Ivy buried her nose in the blooms. "They smell amazing."

Josie wrapped her arms around her younger sister and kissed her on the cheek. "So happy for you, Ivy."

"Has he told his parents yet?" Safia asked.

Ivy looked around nervously not wanting her mother to hear. There was a lot she understood, but much more that she wouldn't. Ivy divulged as little as possible about the expectations of Lut's parents to her own. "Not yet."

"When is he planning to?" Josie asked.

Her sister was easier to talk to than their mother, and Ivy didn't keep any secrets from Josie about anything.

"I'm not sure, but soon."

"*InshaAllah*," Safia added.

"*InshaAllah*," Ivy replied. "I have to remember to start saying that. I keep forgetting."

"Lut will help with that," Safia said. "*InshaAllah*."

"Now you've lost me," Josie interjected. "I'm not savvy to your secret Islamic language yet."

"You'll get used to it," Ivy smiled to her sister.

"*InshaAllah*!" Safia and Ivy shouted in unison, and all three of them burst out in a fit of giggles.

Chapter
19

As it happened, Lut did not need to tell his parents. For some reason after a heated argument with Nazar, Carolyn had picked up the phone and taken the liberty of breaking the news herself.

"Why in the world would she do that?" Ivy asked angrily, moments after Nazar had called Lut to warn him.

"She's crazy," Lut replied. "She has gone completely off the deep end."

Ivy had had no contact with her sister-in-law since their wedding day. Lut spoke to his brother every other weekend, and while Nazar was polite enough to say *Salam* to her and ask how she was before she passed the phone to Lut, her requests to say hello to Carolyn were always met with an excuse about her being out.

"I just don't understand," Ivy said, her anger turning to tears. "What have I done to make her hate me so much?"

"You haven't done anything. She thinks she's trying to save you."

Ivy collapsed onto the couch. "Save me from what?"

"She became a Muslim to marry Nazar. He wouldn't have married her if she hadn't. She did it for the wrong reasons and thinks she's helping you by not allowing you to make the same mistake. Or rather, what she thinks is a mistake."

"That still doesn't make sense, Lut! If she is so unhappy, why doesn't she just leave?"

"And go where?" he asked, unknotting his neck tie and tossing it onto a nearby armchair. "I know her. You don't. She was pregnant with someone else's child when they met. Nazar is the only father Mimi has ever known. Then they had Adam, and now –" He rubbed his hand over his forehead. "Now she is pregnant again."

Ivy's heart sunk. Envy was not an emotion she knew well, but she felt it then. Her wishes of filling her own belly were dashed with each monthly menstrual cycle, three months in a row. Her husband, who had spoken to her more like a doctor than a man reassuring his own wife, told her it took most women approaching thirty up to a year to conceive. His pragmatic approach to the situation did nothing to lessen her pain.

"This is 1985, not 1905," Ivy said. "If she is unhappy she should leave. Unhappy couples get divorced every day. Nazar could still be a father to Mimi and Adam, just not in the same house."

"Nazar will never leave Carolyn as long as she is raising his children. Left to her own devices, those kids would know nothing of Islam."

"That still doesn't explain why she doesn't leave him. Or why they would bring another child into their unhappy marriage?"

"She stays married to Nazar because he isn't a practicing Muslim and probably thinks she can convert him. I don't know, Ivy. I don't know what the hell goes on in that house."

He sat down next to her on the couch and pulled her close. "Please don't ever change."

Guilt crept up in her throat. He had married her knowing she could turn into Carolyn, and by talking about the possibility of divorce she had openly admitted that it was something she herself might consider if their marriage went sour. She couldn't imagine that. Lut was everything she ever wanted. Unlike his brother, Lut was a practicing Muslim and his devotion to their faith only made her own stronger. He was her rock. He helped her grow in her *deen* – Allah's divine purpose for her as expressed in the holy Quran and *hadiths*. Surely if Allah took him from her she would survive, but she would never willingly leave him, and she certainly wouldn't stop being a faithful Muslim without him.

"I was a Muslim before I met you," she whispered. "I will be a Muslim if you are in my life or not. This is what I believe in, in my heart. This is my true faith. I cannot imagine, I would not want, a different way of life."

He relaxed in her embrace and kissed her on the forehead. "I need to call Ammi."

He picked up the phone and made the call, but the exchange between Lut and his mother lasted no more than ten minutes. It was calm on his end, but she had no way of knowing what Ammi's reaction was until he divulged it to her. She sat expectantly as he placed the phone back in its cradle. His smile lifted her heart.

"That was strange," he said.

"What did she –" Ivy started.

He interrupted, "She sounded tired and just said she wanted to come to America."

"It cannot possibly be that easy." Ivy was suspicious. Safia had warned her before she met Lut that this part would probably be explosive. There was no chance in her mind that Lut's mother was perfectly fine with it. There had to be a catch.

It was as if he could read her mind. "She isn't going to tell anyone back home about you until she has come to meet us, and she doesn't want us going there either."

There it was. Ammi wasn't going to acknowledge or accept the marriage until she had scoped it out for herself. To prevent any embarrassment she might be able to nip in the bud, Lut's mother would be lodging herself in their home to make certain the marriage was solid first. Ivy feared for what Ammi would expect of Lut if she didn't find Ivy to be a suitable bride for her youngest son. If Ivy turned out to be another Carolyn.

"She will come with Abbu here first, then go to California to stay with Nazar," he said.

"And Carolyn," she added.

"Yes," he replied."It will be fine, Ivy. She will see that you pray, she will get to know you. She needs this."

"I'm perfectly fine with your parents coming to stay with us, Lut. I'm just afraid she will come with the intent of breaking us up." Ivy's fears slipped right from her lips. She wanted to take it back. The words of their Prophet – peace and blessings be upon him - danced in her head. *Paradise lies at the feet of your mother.* What could be greater evidence of honoring his mother than this? Islam has placed entry to heaven, the ultimate reward, in their devotion to their mothers.

"She won't want to break us up," he assured her. "She's my mother. She wants what is best for me, and she will see with her own eyes that you are what's best for me."

Ivy's mind raced in a thousand different directions. "Why can't she trust that she raised you well enough to know what is best for yourself?"

"She would've with less of a struggle if it wasn't for the mess with Carolyn. Ammi knows how much they fight, because every time Nazar leaves Carolyn calls her for help. Carolyn knows even if Nazar won't listen to her, he will listen to Ammi. She uses Ammi to control him when she can't. That will change when she goes to stay at their house and finds out Carolyn has converted to Christianity."

Ivy was confused. "I thought Muslim men could marry Jewish and Christian women as long as they were practicing. Aren't they *People of the Book*?"

As Muslims, Ivy knew they believed that Allah had previously revealed Himself to Jews and Christians – the *People of the Book* - and Muslims even accepted the teachings of both the Jewish Torah and the Christian Gospels.

Lut started to look flustered. "They are *People of the Book*, but an apostate is different. He didn't marry a chaste, practicing Christian woman, he married a Muslim woman who was pregnant with another man's child, and she became a Christian after. Their marriage isn't even valid Islamically."

Apostasy - the conscious abandonment of Islam by a Muslim - was the sin of all sins. Ivy shivered.

"What will happen when she goes there and sees what is really going on?"

"I don't know, Ivy," he admitted. "But there is a small silver lining for us in all this."

It was an incredible thing for him to say. "How can there possibly be a silver lining in this, Lut?"

"You know I wish my brother every happiness and want only good things for him, but he is old enough to decide his own life and his own path." Lut sat beside her on the couch and took her hand gently. "Ammi and Abbu are coming here first. They will see a happy home and, *inshaAllah*, will have no thought for us at all under the avalanche of problems in California."

It was a horrible concept, someone else's unfortunate circumstances making your own come out better. "I can't think like that Lut, and I don't think you should either. I just want us to be us, to care for your parents while they visit, and to pray for everyone else. I don't want our marriage to be acceptable simply because Nazar and Carolyn's is so bad. I want us all to make it." It was a silly hope in all the madness, but she clung to it all the same.

"You're sweet." Lut smiled. "But you forget this isn't wishing for someone else's failure. This is accepting that their situation is what it is. They are married adults with a family and have to find their own way, just as we have to find ours. We will pray for them, and pray for our parents, and pray for ourselves. We can wish it was different, Ivy, but it isn't – and my concern right now is for my wife and parents. Nazar is a big boy. He can fight his own battles – and Allah knows best."

He was always so practical. Ivy just hoped he was right.

Chapter
20

With the house in order for her in-laws' arrival in a few short hours, Ivy was feeling spectacular. A mixture of excitement and fear swelled in her belly, but the trepidation was more about whether or not Lut's parents would have a comfortable stay over their acceptance of her. She had been well assured by her husband that whatever their response to the marriage was after the visit, he would stay true to her and their wedding vows. He was in this for life, and he loved her.

She knew this to be true without him even saying so, but hearing it from his lips seemed to put everything right in her happy world.

"What's with all the flowers?" Lut asked while she placed at bouquet into its vase and onto the coffee table.

Ivy adjusted a pale yellow bloom that had gone rogue from the bunch. "I love yellow roses. They are so sunny and just radiate joy." She hovered her nose over the spray of flowers. "And they smell wonderful."

"Yes, but do we need them in every room?"

"Most definitely."

Lut had worked a full stretch of ten days at the hospital to get three days off together when his parents arrived. He looked tired, but Ivy didn't miss the glow in his eyes. He was excited for the visit and happy to play host to Ammi and Abbu.

"Nobody will pay much attention to your roses with the beach right there," he teased. "My parents are going to love being so close to the water."

Ivy hadn't heard anything about Lut's parents enjoying the ocean before. "Do they swim?"

Lut burst into laughter. "Swim?" he asked. "I should think not! I cannot imagine Ammi and Abbu splashing around it the waves—although I'd pay to see it!"

Ivy moved towards her husband and wrapped her arms around his waist. "Just walks on the beach then? You think they'll feel at home here, Lut?"

He leaned forward and kissed her on the forehead. "They will, Ivy. I really think they will."

His confidence boosted her own. In her heart she knew once his parents saw how much she and Lut loved one another, how good and happy they were together. there would be nothing that could be levied against them. And the best part was they didn't even have to pretend. They bickered and moaned over small things like any other couple, but their patience and understanding, their mutual respect for each other, that was what carried them the distance.

Ivy picked up the last unbound bouquet of flowers from the countertop before they left the house and headed towards Tampa International. The drive was short and scenic, with the ocean and waterways lining the way into a city of high rises. Tampa didn't boast the skyscrapers of San Francisco, but this particular city by the bay boasted year-round sunshine and a glittering metropolis in the evenings. They rarely ventured out of

Indian Rocks Beach, preferring the small cafes and coffee shops to fancy restaurants, but it was always a delight to drive into the hubbub nonetheless. Lut had settled in comfortably, and she was looking forward to seeing her in-laws do the same, especially on their first visit to America.

The international arrivals gate was packed, everyone trying to get as close to the thin, cabled partition as they could. The doors opened, and streams of new arrivals emerged with their suitcases in tow. Flights from all over the world were landing. While she waited, Ivy made a game of trying to determine which country the surges of passengers were coming from. It was tough to tell. Every time a new influx of people flowed through the doors, they just looked like a bunch of tired Americans returning from vacation. She gave up on the game quickly.

"We should travel more," she said to Lut.

He picked a piece of lint from the elbow of her white linen dress. "Where would you like to go?"

She scanned the crowd and shrugged her shoulders. "Europe, I think. Everyone dreams of Paris, but I've always wanted to see London."

"Isn't England just America with tea and a different accent?"

She smiled at him. "Isn't Pakistan just India with a different religion?"

"Ho-ho-hey now!" he laughed. "Those are fighting words."

Ivy raised her fingers into a mock gun, pulled her thumb down to trigger and blew away the imaginary smoke. Lut flashed a broad grin before jerking his head to the left, catching something from the corner of his eye. Ivy moved in the direction of his gaze and saw two tanned faces in the sea of white. A woman was stylishly attired in a chartreuse *salwar kameez*, her dark hair streaked with hints of white and tucked neatly into a chignon at the nape of her neck. Ammi. Ivy's heart raced in her chest. Behind her walked Abbu, pushing a silver trolley loaded with their luggage.

Lut went quickly to his parents, kissing his mother on both cheeks and taking Abbu's hands from the trolley. "*Assalamualeikum*!"

"*Waleikumsalam*," Ammi replied. Her voice carried the weight of the long journey, exhaustion creeping through her words without affecting the earnest smile she presented her son.

Lut turned halfway around and took his wife by the elbow. "Ammi and Abbu, this is my Ivy."

Ivy stepped forward and met her mother-in-law's smile with one of her own. "*Assalamualeikum*, Ammi and Abbu."

"*Waleikumsalam*," the pair replied, nearly in unison, with Abbu's voice lingering on the M a second longer.

Lut began to speak to his parents in Urdu, pushing the trolley to the airport exit, his parents flanking each side. Ivy followed quietly behind the trio, nearly forgotten when she realized she had dropped her shawl and went back to collect it from the dirty white linoleum. When she raised her eyes, they were already through the glass paneled doors, the electric motor sliding the flaps together with a whirring sound behind them as they proceeded on without her. It was then that she became conscious of the bouquet of flowers she still clutched in her shaking hand.

The ride back was filled with foreign chatter, Lut occasionally pointing out the window to views of the waterways. Ivy's heart sunk when Ammi turned to her briefly and gave little more than a forced, tight-lipped half-smile. When Ammi's head tilted back towards the window, Ivy reached over and gently wrapped her fingers around her mother-in-law's. Ammi's hand stiffened, but she didn't recoil. She turned her face back, and they locked eyes. Ivy took a deep breath and tried her best to piece together some of the little Urdu she knew into something that Ammi might understand. "*Zayada pareshan na hoon, inshaAllah. Sub theek ho jahay ga.*"

Everything is going to be all right, inshaAllah. Please don't be too upset.

She spoke louder than she had meant to, and the car went silent. Ammi's fingers relaxed and she raised her other hand to pat the top of Ivy's. Her eyes registered a mixture of surprise and understanding, and the tightness around her mouth softened into a sad smile. "*InshaAllah.*"

To Ivy, Ammi's momentary thawing was slight victory. She would continue to carefully chisel away the premature, rocky relationship that was inevitable between a mother who had been blindsided by her son, and the woman who carried the burden of proof that it wouldn't be another disaster.

Chapter
21

    The first few days with the new family in the house were quiet. Ivy spent much of her days preparing meals with Ammi—meals Safia had taught her—while Abbu took long walks along the beach. Ivy made an effort to talk to her in-laws and was pleasantly surprised by their firm grasp of the English language, a necessity when Lut returned to the hospital after the first week. Abbu was easy to please with the kind weather and plates laden with hearty curries. He smiled frequently and spoke little, but Lut assured her this was just his way. He had never been a man of many words and was gratified by the simplest of pleasures.

Ammi's temperament had also warmed under the Florida sun, and Ivy was beginning to feel comfortable, at ease even, in her presence. It had happened quicker than she had hoped, and Lut had relayed to her the kind things Ammi had said.

"She was surprised that you pray five times a day. That was important for her to see." he had told her. "And that you really look after me. All of us."

It hadn't been difficult. There was no change to Ivy's daily routine, just the addition of a hot lunch in the afternoons and larger portions for breakfast and dinner. Two extra cups of tea before Lut left in the mornings wasn't exactly a terrible inconvenience. "She knew I prayed. You already told her that before they came. Is that all she said?"

"I had told her before, but Nazar had claimed something similar about Carolyn, so telling her that wasn't going to mean much. It was important that she saw it. She likes your temperament, said you are a naturally happy person. She hasn't been sold on you completely yet, but you are definitely winning her over…just by being you."

Ivy took her husband's encouragement and allowed it to soothe over any lingering anxiety she felt. She had no problem just being herself, which included a cheerful temperament. She had nothing in her life to be ungrateful for, praise be to Allah. She was blessed with a comfortable home, a husband who adored her, and a family of her own—her parents and sister—who were as supportive and loving as any person could wish for. "When should we introduce them to my family? They know your parents are here and I can't continue to make excuses."

"This weekend would be good. Invite them over. Ammi has been asking about them anyway."

This had surprised Ivy a little. "She asked about my parents?"

"You know how important family is. They need to meet yours as much as Jim and Dorothy need to meet them."

Ivy laughed imagining her father in the same room with calm, unassuming Abbu. "It will be interesting to see how they take to my dad. He's always been the bull in the china shop."

"I'm not about to try and tame that bull, but I will have to warn Ammi that he can be…thunderous. Your dad is loads of fun. Just, you know, kind of…loud."

Ivy smiled, shaking away the memory of their conversation. She still had to call her parents and invite them over. Ammi and Abbu were sitting on the patio in a pair of rattan chairs they had claimed as their own. Ammi was staring off toward the ocean, and Abbu had nodded off to sleep. The thick double glazing of the sliding glass doors made his loud snoring undetectable to Ivy in the kitchen. Ammi had clearly become immune to it.

She picked up the phone and waited for her mother to answer. "Hello?"

"Hi Mom, how are you?"

"I'm doing great darling, just about to meet Josie for lunch. Do you want to join us?"

Ivy's eyes rested on her in-laws on the porch. She missed the last two lunches she had been invited to with her mom and sister. They were always so carefree and easy. She wanted to say yes but knew it was impossible. "Not today, Mom. But I was calling to invite you and Dad over for lunch on Saturday. Can you make it?"

"We sure can, honey. Are we finally going to meet Lut's parents? Seems a bit strange they've been here a week and we haven't seen hide nor hair of them."

"I'm sorry, Mom. We just wanted them to adjust to the time difference and find their bearings here. It's a big change, Lahore to Tampa. It's a long way to travel."

"You don't have to explain that to me, Ivy. I used to get tired driving to Orlando—and that's only an hour away."

Those drives to Walt Disney World always felt as long as any trans-Atlantic flight. It's a terrible thing to be a child in the back seat of a station wagon, counting down the seconds until she could see Mickey and Minnie Mouse with their arms spread on each side of that glorious, yellow flagged, arched sign. Walt Disney World. The Happiest Celebration on Earth. "Can you come at one?"

"Daddy and I will be there with bells and whistles."

Ivy paused for a moment, knowing her mother could mean that literally.

"Just kidding, honey. Should we bring anything?"

"Just a smile."

"Well, that's easy enough. How about Josie? Is she invited?"

"Not this time, Mom. I think it's best if they just meet you first."

Her mother let out a sigh. "This is all a bit strange, Ivy. Josie is your sister."

Ivy looped her finger through the curl of the phone cord. Her mother was always so funny about including Josie where Josie definitely was not interested in being included. There was a mother-daughter camaraderie there that had always been present in only their mother's mind. At Disney World, her mother had frequently called them "The Three Mouseketeers" and dubbed their father as Goofy. Josie and Ivy secretly rolled their eyes at each other. Why would they want to be Mouseketeers with Mom when Cinderella and Sleeping Beauty were present? "It isn't a big deal. I'll call her and if she seems out of sorts I'll extend the invite, but you know Josie. She's not going to care. I wouldn't exactly be jumping through hoops to try and meet her in-laws."

The quiet on the other end confirmed that her mother wasn't convinced. "See you Saturday at one, Mom."

She put the phone back in its cradle and, after giving her pot of lentils and lamb a good stir, went to sit with Ammi and Abbu under the glorious sun. When Lut got home that evening, she decided she was going to press him to take them all to Walt Disney World on his next day off. She was certain Ammi and Abbu could use a day at The Happiest Celebration on Earth.

Chapter 23

The loud knock came at one o'clock sharp, and Lut ushered Ivy's parents into the house to where his parents stood stoically in the living room.

"Well hello there," her dad nearly shouted, extending his hand to either Ammi or Abbu. It was unclear who he was reaching for. "Nice to finally meet the parents of such a fine young man!"

Abbu graciously shook Jim's hand, and Ammi nodded her head gracefully at him. She was, as always, a picture of elegance in a beaded maroon sari. She wore it in a fashion that reflected her observance to Islam, with long sleeves and without the traditional showing of stomach flesh. She looked positively regal.

"These are my parents, Dorothy and Jim. Mom and Dad, this is Ammi and Abbu."

Her mom reached out towards Ammi and put her hand on her elbow, leaning in. "It is just lovely to meet you, Ammi."

Ammi smiled politely. "Please do call me Aalia. Ammi is just what the children call me. And my husband is called Rashid."

Ivy was taken aback. Aalia? Rashid? How was it possible that she had never known her own in-laws' real names before this moment? She looked at Lut, who leaned in to chuckle in her ear. "It's a good sign, Ammi not asking to be called Mrs. Miah."

"Aalia?" she mouthed back, still stunned at the revelation. Lut winked. She turned her attention back to the odd pairing of parents in front of her.

Her mother, it appeared, was attempting to channel Jackie Onassis in a tweed yellow jacket, pencil skirt, and a string of pearls around her slender neck. She gently pulled a pin from a matching box cap and set it on the coffee table. Next to her, Ivy's dad was in a collared shirt she was certain her mother had forced upon him. It was tucked into the waist of his blue jeans. He must've put his foot down at wearing a belt.

"Can I take your jacket, Mom?"

She looked to her nervously and shook her head *no*. "I think I'll keep it on."

There was no way she was comfortable in a tweed coat, no matter how light it was. "Are you sure, let me just…"

Her father cleared his throat. Ivy understood his hint and let it drop, while Lut motioned the parents to the couches.

Her dad lingered behind and whispered to Ivy, "She forgot about not showing too much skin and has nothing but a white tank top under that jacket. It's a fancy one, but it's still a tank. She meant well, just slipped her mind I guess."

Ivy nodded. She knew what to do. "Thanks Daddy. It wouldn't bother anyone, but I don't want Mom to feel out of place either."

"That's a good girl."

Just as her mother went to sit, Ivy asked, "Mom, just for a moment, can I get your opinion on something upstairs?"

Her mother looked confused. "Now?"

Ivy nodded *yes* and, reluctantly, her mother rose and followed her upstairs. She had plenty of white blouses that her mom would find more comfortable than a tweed jacket.

Once changed into an airy cap-sleeved blouse, they rejoined the party in the living room and her mother made a show of removing her Jackie O jacket. "Well, I do think I will have you take this, Ivy honey."

It was rare for Ivy to see her mother in heels and pantyhose. The look suited her, even if she they all knew she was supposed to leave the yellow pumps at the door. They did, after all, pray on the living room floor occasionally. "Tea, anyone?"

"Coffee for me," her dad replied.

Her mom settled in next to Ammi on the love seat. "Tea would be nice."

Ammi nodded in agreement.

"So how are you finding the states?" her mom asked. Her voice was a little too high, and she drew out the words just a bit too slowly. She'd have to remind her mom that Ammi's English was fine, and she certainly wasn't deaf.

Ammi maintained her composure and answered so softly that Ivy couldn't hear what she had to say from the kitchen. It appeared to not take her mom long at all to fall into a comfortable, even toned chat with Ammi. She took in the sight of her husband, his parents, and her parents all together in the same space. It was not a sight she expected so soon but was wonderfully happy about it.

The luncheon proceeded without a hitch. Abbu did his level best to keep up with Lut and Ivy's dad's banter, and the women kept the conversation to polite and respectable topics of the weather, the beach, which seafood restaurants they must try, and the best hair products to combat Florida's humidity. Later in the afternoon when they had returned home, her mom called to tell Lut that his parents were a delight and that she would love to take them all out to one of the restaurants she had recommended.

Ammi was just as complimentary, and Ivy saw an animated side to her mother-in-law that she knew only the affability of her own parents would've procured. "Wonderful people, *mashaAllah*."

Ivy was up to her elbows in dish soap. "They had the same to say about you, Ammi."

"It is very different here than at home." She twisted the gold band around her finger. "People are more open. More friendly. Is it always like this?"

Ivy wiped her hands on a dish towel and turned to face Ammi. "Friendly and polite are not the same thing, as I'm sure you know. Americans are friendly but not very reserved. Sometimes, to some people who aren't familiar with it, it might come across as…I don't know. Not altogether too polite."

"*Ahan*. I see."

"I think politeness is all relative to where you are in the world. What is polite here might not be polite in Lahore. What is friendly in Lahore might not be considered very friendly here."

"I think your parents—I think you—are polite and friendly in all places. In Lahore and here, *mashaAllah*."

Ivy gripped the dish towel in her hand. It was all she could do to keep from throwing her arms around Ammi and drowning the aging woman in her own delight. "*JazakAllah*, Ammi. Thank you so, so much."

235

Chapter
23

On the last day before they boarded their flight to California, Ivy and Lut packed both sets of parents and Josie into a rented minivan and made their way to Disney World. Dorothy hadn't been since the opening of EPCOT Center and had decided they should all visit that park, as it would be a new experience for everyone. Ivy had agreed easily, unable to imagine Ammi and Abbu on any of the Magic Kingdom rides.

It had been a blissful month for them all, dotted throughout with frequent lunches and outings between the two mothers and Ivy. Ammi and Dorothy had even gone off alone for afternoon manicures in Tampa after an extravagant seafood lunch at the Colonnade Restaurant, which boasted sweeping views of the Hillsborough Bay.

Ivy was grateful for her mother's keen interest in fine dining and entertaining. Ivy herself enjoyed it, but she hadn't planned for a mother-in-law who took such pleasure in being a socialite. Ammi and Ivy's mother made a peculiar pair to anyone observing them from neighboring tables, but beneath it all the women were both thriving patricians—the "ladies who lunch" lifestyle suiting them equally. Ivy's father had grumbled to Ivy at first, pointing out that the lifestyle wasn't equal as Lut's parents were rich and hers were not. He stopped commenting altogether when Ivy offered to help finance her mother's outings, which he promptly refused.

During their time at home, Ivy enjoyed quiet afternoons with her in-laws. Ammi had taught her to cook *haleem*, a dish Lut had claimed as his favorite but was too time consuming for Ivy to master. Her basmati rice no longer stuck to the sides of the pan and separated perfectly for her *biryani* on Ammi's suggestion of adding white vinegar to the water. They prayed together, walked together on the beach, discussed religion and politics— of which Ivy politely agreed on even when she didn't— and shared stories about Lut, Ammi about his past, Ivy about his present. To Ivy's disappointment, there were two things Ammi would not discuss. The first was anything regarding her migration to Pakistan during the Partition of India, which Ivy knew from her time at university, must have been a harrowing, bloody ordeal. The second was Lut's aunt and uncle, Fatima and Imran.

"No, I cannot." she would say, waving her hand briskly in front of her. It was clear any mention of either topic was the source of great pain. Ivy always conceded and moved on to things Ammi was content to discuss, such as her oldest son Safwat and his enchanting wife Iqra.

Ivy felt she had bonded with Lut's mother, and was even so bold as to admit to herself she had won her over. She knew this to be true when Ammi spoke to Safwat in Pakistan and gave him permission to make Ivy and Lut's marriage known. It was decided that when they returned, the couple would go to Lahore for a formal *walima*. In her mind, Ivy was already imagining the celebration. But for today, today they would be hosted by none other than Mickey Mouse.

"I will not put that on!" Ammi said, covering her neat coiffure with her hands as Ivy's mother and Lut attempted to put a pair of Mickey ears on her head.

Ivy's mom would have none of it. "It's just a headband, Aalia! You have to wear one! It's Disney World!"

Ivy put the mouse ears on her own head and walked over to her mom and Ammi. "Just for a minute, Ammi. Just for one picture."

Ammi laughed and reluctantly agreed. The three women, all in mouse ears, smiled at Lut and his camera. The shutter clicked, and Ivy's mother clapped her hands excitedly. "The Three Mouseketeers!"

It was a photo Ivy would treasure forever after.

Six weeks later, in the middle of the night, they received the call that Ammi had died of a heart attack.

The Dog Bride

There was once a young man who used to herd buffaloes. Day in and day out, he watched his animals graze and came to notice a she-dog make her way to a ravine every day at high noon. The man's curiosity was piqued, and he wondered: "To whom does she belong? What does she do in the ravine?

One morning, the man hid himself in the ravine until noon when the she-dog came. He was amazed to see that when she got to the pools of water at the bottom of the ravine, she shed her dog skin, and out stepped a beautiful maiden who began to bathe. The man watched the captivating maiden in the pools, and when she had finished bathing, she put on the she-dog skin and went off to the village. The man followed her to see what house she entered, and inquired to whom the house belonged. Once he knew, he went back to his work.

Later in the year the young man's parents decided that it was time for him to marry and began to look about for a wife for him. The young man would have none of it and announced that he had made up his mind to have a dog for a wife—that he would never marry a human girl.

The man was laughed at by everyone he knew and even those he didn't, but he could not be moved. Finally, his parents conceded that their son must have the soul of a dog, and it was best to let him have his own way. His parents asked him whether there was any particular dog he would like to have for his bride, and he promptly gave the name of the man into whose house he had tracked the she-dog from the ravine. The master of the dog laughed at the idea that anyone should wish to marry her, but he gladly accepted the parents' bride price. The day was fixed for the wedding and the booth built for the ceremony. The bridegroom's party collected the she-dog, the marriage took place in due form, and the bride was escorted afterward to her husband's house.

Every night when her husband was asleep, the bride used to come out of the she-dog's skin and leave the house. When her husband discovered this, he pretended to go to sleep one night and lay watching her. She was about to leave the room when he jumped up, seized the discarded she-dog skin, and threw it into the fire where it was burnt to ashes. After this, his bride remained the beautiful woman of the ravine, her magnificence and grace far beyond anything human. The bride was happy to be free, and was dutiful and loving to her husband. This soon became known in the village, and everyone congratulated the young man on his wisdom in marrying a dog.

The young man had a cousin, and when he saw what a prize his cousin had got, he thought that he could not do better than marry a she-dog himself. After his cousin's success, there were no objections, even though his cousin warned that his bride was special. He knew what she really was before marriage, and only changed physically after. This was rare, he warned, and almost impossible to find. The cousin's advice was ignored, and a bride was selected. The marriage took place, but when they were putting vermilion on the bride's forehead, she began to growl. In spite of that, they dragged her to the bridegroom's house and forcibly anointed her with oil and turmeric. When the bride's party set off home, the dog broke loose and ran after them. Everyone shouted to the bridegroom to run after his bride and bring her back, but she only snarled and bit at him. At last, he had no choice but to give up. The villagers all laughed at him so much that he was too ashamed to speak, having ignored his cousin's warning and married an unknown she-dog instead. Three days later, knowing no respected family would ever marry their daughter to such an impulsive fool, he hanged himself.

Chapter
24

Carolyn
1986 - San Francisco Bay Area, California

The marriage had been crumbling before
Ammi's death. Cracks in their relationship that widened,
fragments of a broken marriage crumbling around them.
It had been slow at first, beginning with the fight where
she had struck him. There had been more clashes, and
the more frequently they happened, the less Carolyn felt

in control of her temper. Her tirades had worsened, and she didn't recognize herself anymore. She hated how calm he was when she felt her own rage bubbling over. She found it to be condescending, like he was manipulating her with patience to make her feel—to look—unreasonable.

She brushed a stray lock of hair off her face and secured the claw at the back her necklace, admiring her reflection in the mirror. "I'm not unreasonable. I'm just miserable."

There was one place she felt solace, and in Father Michael she had found a confidante. With him, in the Parish, she was at peace. He had taught her to pray again, both the prescribed prayers of old in Latin and the ones that poured naturally from her own heart.

Nazar had started to pray again also. Not five times a day as he had in Lahore, but on Fridays for Jummah, in the masjid Lut had attended before he moved to Florida. When she first started to wear the cross around her neck, he seemed indifferent, too exhausted to start a fresh fight over a tired topic. He was less patient when he discovered she was attending daily mass with Mimi and the son Nazar wanted raised Muslim in her belly.

"You can go to the church, but you cannot bring my children," he had said.

She shrugged. "That's fine. Mimi can stay home by herself while I go then. She's potty trained now so she'll be all right."

"It isn't a joke, Carolyn. I'm serious."

"She's too young to understand anything. We'll figure it out when she's older."

He conceded and let the matter drop.

When Adam had been born, there was a brief period of calm. They were enraptured by their son, they pushed their troubles aside until sleepless nights and postpartum depression forced the fractures in their marriage to resurface and began crushing her under an avalanche of despair. She returned to the church with both children and had Father Michael baptize her son in the name of Adam—the name she and Nazar had agreed on, in a Catholic sacrament he would never have allowed. It was kept a secret for a few days until Mimi made an innocent mention of it. The memory of it was still fresh in Carolyn's mind.

"Adam got to play in the special water, but he didn't like it. He cried. I didn't cry."

Nazar turned to Carolyn, his brows furrowing in confusion. "Did you take them to a pool?"

Carolyn opened her mouth to respond, but Mimi beat her to it. "No, Daddy! The Jesus water isn't a pool! It's too small!"

"The *what* water?"

In her excitement, Mimi carried on. "The water so we can be with Jesus when we go to heaven! Can we go to a real pool though?"

"Not today, peanut," Carolyn said. "Why don't you put your PJ's on."

The moment Mimi was out of sight, Nazar looked as if ready to explode. He kept his voice low. "You had better tell me right now what you have done."

"Adam was baptized. It was important to me, and he will never remember. Because you don't think it means anything, it shouldn't matter to you."

"Are you out of your mind, Carolyn? It shouldn't matter to me that my kids have been baptized as Christians? "

"Catholic," she corrected him. "And Mimi isn't your kid."

Carolyn heard a high-pitched wail behind her. *Please God don't let her have heard me say that. Why did I say that?*

Still screaming, Mimi ran past her to Nazar and wrapped her arms around his legs. "He's my daddy! He's my daddy!"

Nazar glared at Carolyn and picked the sobbing girl up in his arms. He stroked her hair and whispered in her ear. "I'm your daddy, baby. I'm your daddy."

He brushed past Carolyn to console Mimi in her room.

"We'll discuss this another time," he told Carolyn.

But they never did discuss it, and like everything else, Nazar let it drop. That was how their marriage went, and Carolyn could only chalk it up to her husband not wanting stress or conflict in his life. They argued, and sometimes the arguments led to Carolyn losing her temper completely. Sometimes she struck him, lashing out with her arms where her words seemed to have no effect on him. She always regretted it afterward but couldn't seem to control her anger with him. Nazar never pushed back, and that infuriated her even more. The worst was when he left, and she feared he might not return—but he always did—usually after the second or third night, when she'd reach the height of panic and call Ammi for help. Ammi always knew where to reach him, and Nazar would walk through the door within a few hours of her desperate call to Pakistan. They'd have heated, passionate make-up sex, discuss nothing, and carry on as though there hadn't been a fight.

But now Ammi was gone.

Her death had shaken Nazar to the core, and he had left in haste to bury his mother in Lahore. With only two months to go until she was due to give birth to her third child, Carolyn was relieved when the doctor advised against her accompanying her husband to Pakistan. Mimi and Adam had also stayed behind. Adam didn't have a passport, and even if he had, Nazar was too overcome with grief to look after two small children on such a strenuous journey. He had collapsed after receiving the call from Safwat that Ammi was gone, weeping like a small child himself in her arms. Her heart ached for his loss. For his pain.

In the week since he left, Carolyn continued attending mass daily with Mimi and Adam in tow. This routine had not changed even when Ammi and Abbu had come for their month-long visit, and she no longer felt the need to hide her faith from anyone—including Nazar's family.

She had even consulted with Father Michael about Ammi's death, and he had assured her that her mother-in-law might still not be relegated to hellfire, even as a Muslim. He recited to her a translated section of the Vatican's Lumen Gentium:

The non-Christian may not be blamed for his ignorance of Christ and his Church; salvation is open to him also, if he seeks God sincerely and if he follows the commands of his conscience, for through this means the Holy Ghost acts upon all men; this divine action is not confined within the limited boundaries of the visible Church.

There were no guarantees with salvation, but Carolyn found comfort in the possibilities extended through the grace of God. Through the words of the church. Her church.

She could hardly believe Ammi was gone. She had sat on their sofa only two weeks before, drinking chai, coddling Adam, and giving Carolyn stern looks every time she noticed the cross around her neck. Ammi said nothing to Carolyn directly about her obvious apostasy and instead treated the same way her son did—

by ignoring the possibility that it occurred under her own nose. What she did talk about was her visit to Florida and all the wonderful virtues of her other daughter-in-law, Ivy. Ivy was gentle and kind. Ivy was nurturing and loving. Ivy and Lut never fought openly. Ivy came from a solid family, unbroken by divorce, her parents being such a part of her life. Ivy was a perfect host.

But the compliment that grated Carolyn the most...

Ivy was just like Iqra.

Ammi filled the air with so much praise for her two golden daughters that the atmosphere of Carolyn's home became dense with conviction of her own inferiority. She could feel it suffocating her.

Nazar claimed it wasn't intentional. He insisted his mother wasn't implying Carolyn was bad, just that her time with Ivy and Iqra was pleasant. "She's had a lot of sadness in her life and enjoys talking about happier times."

She always bristled at this defense. "You would never say anything against your mother."

"There's nothing to say. She loved being in Florida. Why can't she talk about it?"

"Why can't she talk about anything else?"

"She has nothing else to talk about. You've seen how closeted her life is in Lahore. Let the woman chatter happily about my brother's wives and her travels. You're making a big deal out of nothing."

She was always accused of making a big deal out of nothing, her feelings and concerns so easily discarded for the sake of appeasing others. Hadn't she shown Ammi and Abbu all the best the Bay Area had to offer? She had taken them to San Francisco, snapped their photos on the Golden Gate Bridge, and walked them through the magnificent rotunda at the Palace of Fine Arts. They had taken the trolley cars to a seaside restaurant that served fresh crab legs on Fisherman's Wharf and had chocolate sundaes in Ghirardelli Square.

"Does Ammi talk to Ivy and Iqra about the things she is doing here?"

Nazar smiled and reached his hand out to her. She took it and relished in her husband's affection. "She went on and on to Iqra about the fat, lazy seals by the pier. Did Mimi force her onto a merry-go-round?"

"It didn't take much force." She laughed. "Mimi has her grandma wrapped around her little finger."

"I would've liked to have seen that. I'm sorry I couldn't make it."

"It's ok. There's loads of pictures."

"You're being a great host, Carolyn. It's not a competition." He put his hand on her belly. "And even if it was, you're the only one who has given them grandsons."

She rested her head on his shoulder. "Granddaughters count too, and she has Mimi and little Zara." Ammi had proudly shown her photos of Iqra and Safwat's daughter—a daughter they had allowed Ammi to name.

"Yes, granddaughters count too. But let's let the numbers speak for themselves. Once this little boy is born, you'll be mother to three quarters of their grandchildren."

"God bless them all," Carolyn whispered.

Nazar had stiffened under her slightly. "*Alhamdullilah*," he said, a little too sternly for Carolyn's comfort.

The morning Ammi and Abbu were leaving for the airport, Carolyn had walked into a living room full of sad, tired eyes. The coffee table was still littered with dessert plates from the evening before, the sticky residue of store-bought baklava flickering under the early morning light. She knew Nazar had been up talking to his parents all night. When nobody met her eyes or said a word to her as she collected the dirty dishes, she also knew it was unlikely their discussion had been about how wonderful they all thought she was.

After Nazar returned from the airport, he was too tired to talk. Carolyn wanted so badly to leave it alone, but the mounting panic in her throat pushed her to force a conversation her husband didn't want to have.

"Tell me what you were talking about all night."

Nazar went to the bed and pulled the covers up to his ears. "Nothing you need to worry about, Carolyn."

"Tell me now or I will take the kids and go."

He pulled the comforter over his head. "I hadn't seen my parents for years. I don't know when I will see them again. I'm upset, I'm very tired, and I am going to sleep."

She knew he was telling a part truth, but she also knew there was more. "Nobody said anything to me this morning, Nazar. That's not normal."

Nazar threw the sheet from over his head and sat up. His eyes were red from crying and his voice shook. "They kissed you goodbye, Carolyn. They hugged and kissed you. Did you want a song and dance? Did you want them to touch your feet? The only thing that isn't normal here is this conversation. None of our conversations are ever normal. Now get off the bed, leave me alone, and let me get some sleep."

His words cut her and she knew—she *knew*—he spoke only in anger. But her own frustration boiled. Just as she opened her mouth to allow her heart to release itself, she was interrupted by one of the few sounds that could shake her from a rage.

"Mommy, I'm hungry." Mimi stood at the door clutching a stuffed bear Ammi had given her just before leaving.

"I'll be right there, peanut."

Nazar sunk back into the bed and pulled the sheets back over his head. Carolyn rested her hand on his shoulder. "I'm just..." she started. "I don't think you are telling me everything."

He shifted slightly but didn't pull away from her touch. "If you think we talked about the cross around your neck, you're right. But they didn't do anything but ask what was going on and what was going to happen with our kids. You need to trust me, Carolyn. They're confused. I'm confused, and we have to talk about it. But right now, I need to sleep."

She had left him to get Mimi cereal, and like all the times before, the conversation they so desperately needed to have never happened. The problems they had mounting against them were buried under the sheets with her snoring husband.

The call that Ammi died came two weeks later and Nazar, broken and bewildered, left to lay his mother to rest.

Chapter
25

"How are you?" She knew the answer would be fine, even though he wasn't.

Nazar let out a sigh. His voice crackled through the phone as if he were speaking into a tin can. "Fine."

He had been gone for nearly ten days. Carolyn had felt able to breathe clearly—think clearly—for the first time in months. "When are you coming back?"

"The day after tomorrow."

He had taken the car to the airport and parked it in long term. She knew he wasn't expecting her to meet him. "Good."

"All right.Well, I'll see you when I get home."

Carolyn stayed quiet, fingering the cross at her neck. *O God, grant me the serenity...*

"Listen, Carolyn. I love you."

To accept the things I cannot change, the courage to change the things I can...

"I can't wait to hold you and the kids."

And the wisdom to know the difference.

"Everything will be fine, Carolyn."

She brought the cross to her lips. "I know it will. Have a safe flight."

"Bye, baby."

"Goodbye, Nazar."

Carolyn set the phone down and walked over to the door where her suitcases stood. Adam was asleep in his carrier, and Mimi was struggling to get her arm into her coat. Carolyn bent down, smiled at her daughter, and once her little arm was secure, she zipped the front of the jacket.

She folded the note she'd written Nazar and set it on the countertop as a horn honked impatiently from the parking lot below.

Mimi had her hands on a bright yellow suitcase and was walking in circles around it, her fingers not lifting from the handle. "Are we going far, Mommy?"

"We're going far, peanut."

"Are we going long, Mommy?"

"We'll be gone for long, peanut. Yes."

"Is Daddy gonna come too?"

"No Mimi. Daddy isn't coming."

She picked up Adam's carrier and took Mimi's hand, opening the door for the taxi driver to collect their bags. Before she followed him out, she took a final look back behind her and closed the door. Then she locked it and dropped the keys through the mail slot. She never looked back.

1. Whispers from the East has three point of view characters. Between Ammi, Carolyn, and Ivy, which did you connect most with? Why?

2. Are the characters or their circumstances familiar to you in any way? If so, how? If not, can you empathize with them?

3. Do you feel as if this book changed your views on the primary subject of the story? Why?

4. The adherence to different social customs of all three main characters can seem controversial to us today. Pick a scene where you would have acted differently. Why?

5. Do the characters react the way you think you would in a similar situation? Do you find their actions troubling?

6. The book starts by telling us Ammi has died of a heart attack. Knowing this from the onset, were you surprised by the ending? How did you expect it to end?

7. Do you feel 'changed' in any way? Did the book expand your range of experience or challenge your

assumptions (for example, did it take you to a place you haven't been before or help you see people you know in a different light)?

8. What do you think will happen to Ivy and Carolyn next? Do you think the author has planned a sequel, or left their endings up to you?

9. If you could change the ending of this book, how would you end it and why?

10. Overall, did you like the book or not? Did you enjoy it? Why or why not?

www.ingramcontent.com/pod-product-compliance
Lightning Source LLC
Chambersburg PA
CBHW031707170626
46808CB00005B/1643